the

WEIGHT

of

the

SKY

the WEIGHT of the SKY

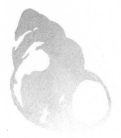

LISA ANN SANDELL

Viking

𝒱iking

Published by Penguin Group

Penguin Young Readers Group, 345 Hudson Street, New York, New York 10014, U.S.A.
Penguin Group (Canada), 90 Eglinton Avenue East, Suite 700, Toronto, Ontario,
Canada M4P 2Y3 (a division of Pearson Penguin Canada Inc.)
Penguin Books Ltd, 80 Strand, London WC2R 0RL, England
Penguin Ireland, 25 St Stephen's Green, Dublin 2, Ireland
(a division of Penguin Books Ltd)
Penguin Group (Australia), 250 Camberwell Road, Camberwell, Victoria 3124,
Australia (a division of Pearson Australia Group Pty Ltd)
Penguin Books India Pvt Ltd, 11 Community Centre, Panchsheel Park,
New Delhi – 110 017, India
Penguin Group (NZ), Cnr Airborne and Rosedale Roads, Albany,
Auckland 1310, New Zealand (a division of Pearson New Zealand Ltd)
Penguin Books (South Africa) (Pty) Ltd, 24 Sturdee Avenue, Rosebank,
Johannesburg 2196, South Africa

Penguin Books Ltd, Registered Offices: 80 Strand, London WC2R 0RL, England

First published in 2006 by Viking, a division of Penguin Young Readers Group

1 3 5 7 9 10 8 6 4 2

LIBRARY OF CONGRESS CATALOGING-IN-PUBLICATION DATA
Sandell, Lisa Ann, date–
The weight of the sky / by Lisa Ann Sandell.
p. cm.
Summary: A sixteen-year-old girl travels to Israel to spend the summer on a kibbutz
and discovers who she is and what she wants out of life.
ISBN 0-670-06028-3
1. Jews—United States—Juvenile fiction. [1. Jews—United States—Fiction.
2. Coming of age—Fiction. 3. Kibbutzim—Fiction. 4. Israel—Fiction.] I. Title.
PZ7.S19746Wei 2006   [Fic]—dc22   2005007341

Set in Berkeley
Book design by Nancy Brennan

To Carolyn Kim and Charlotte Sheedy
countless thanks for your fiercely devoted guidance and enthusiasm
for your unflagging support, nurturing, and love
for allowing me to place my blind trust in you

To Catherine Frank
with deepest gratitude for your insightful and perceptive editing
for your patience, passion, and grace
for your willingness to take a chance on me

To George Ney
undying thanks, my dear friend, for all the coffee,
conversation, advice, and love
for giving me a home away from home all these years

For Mom, Dad, and Sharon
I will never be able to stop thanking you
for your endless love, wisdom, humor, faith, and encouragement
I couldn't have done this without you—I love you

For Liel
my loyal reader, my loving teacher
my most beloved friend and guide
you are cherished, my love, my heart, my light, my life

the WEIGHT of the SKY

THE AIRPLANE

I peer outside the tiny,
scratched-up window and
exhale a foggy mist,
clouding the glass,
blocking the view.
There is no view, anyway.
Blue sky blends seamlessly
with blue sea,
and I don't know if it's my blue mood
coloring the scenery,
but apprehension fills me
as I sit here.
Waiting.
Waiting for the plane to land.
I took off from New York on a
balmy summer afternoon.
The kind that's filled with mosquitoes and
still, heavy air
and sweat that won't evaporate

until the stale air-conditioning of a jet
dries it away.

Yes, I'm Tel Aviv–bound.
That's what a nice girl like me
is doing on a big airplane
all by herself,
going away
for the first time
alone.
I wished for an exotic voyage to
wipe clean the calendar of
dull days,
each one identical to
the day that came before it,
and the one that follows.
But now,
now I'm frightened.

A child's cry fractures
the near silence of sleepers.
And the men in the black hats and cloaks
      Hasids
      Orthodox Jews
gather in the rear of the airplane

for their daily morning prayers.

Stroking their long, unruly beards,

these men, who appear to be from

the eighteenth century,

with their breeches and white stockings,

are foreign and absurd

on a jumbo jet.

But there's comfort, too,

a familiarity.

I mean, I've watched *Fiddler on the Roof*.

And my mother made sure I understood

that those Jews depicted in their

little Russian shtetl

were my family's heritage, too.

Quietly the men argue

until they settle on a direction to face

  of Jerusalem

  and the fallen Temple

while they pray.

They bend at the knees and waist,

beards and hats tipping,

as they,

in ecstasy of communion with God,

thank the Lord

for waking them up.

The murmur of chanting,
at once mournful and untidy,
soon drowned out by the voices
echoing in my head:
Sarah, when are you going
to get serious about your college applications?
Sarah, are you ready
for the Ivy interviews?
Sarah, this is no joke!

I open my eyes.
Stomach still turning.
Wisps of clouds brush
past the window,
over the wings.
And parents' voices fade
to an indistinct humming.

The airplane has begun its descent.
As we pull free
of the sheath of white mist,
the sea opens up beneath us.
Then
        shoreline, pale beaches, and seafoam waves.
My first glimpse of the land.

We're old souls, this country and I.
I visit her in my dreams,
this dusty land crowned by mountains and desert.
      The empty places, where I feel free.

The pilot's thick accent cuts through the
loudspeaker, welcoming us to Israel.
A Hebrew folk song blares
to the accompaniment
of tears (mine)
and hand-clapping
(the others).
We leave the plane in a rush,
running down the stairs,
met with a blast of heat and sun,
pushing and shuffling to get in a line.
And the girl at the passport-control counter
in a dark green military-style uniform
startles me
with her surliness.
She's not much older than I.
      Her eyes, deep-set and muddy,
        could have been mine.
The leather strap of my bag
digs in, makes its mark,

searing red,
on my shoulder.
The girl's eyes challenge mine,
daring them to hold her gaze.
The purpose of my visit, I tell her,
     staring back
     then looking down,
is to volunteer on a kibbutz.
My passport is stamped with a resounding
THUMP
and I'm on my way.

REMEMBERING, PART 1

THUMP
My mother dropped a handful
of pamphlets on the table.
"Come to Israel!"
"Come to a kibbutz!"
"Explore your roots!"
Thirty brochures splayed in front of me
as I was trying to do my math homework.
Angles and triangles and balls going up
and falling down,
speed and height,
none of it making any sense to me.
Yet.
I always get it eventually,
        being one of those "Smart Jews."
What is this? I asked.
I could feel her standing there
behind me
waiting.

Well, it's your birthday present, Sarah.
Happy birthday. She paused
and sighed.
I can't believe you're sixteen.
Dad and I decided you should go to Israel
this summer. Explore your roots,
as they say.
Gee, Mom, thanks. I mustered up my
most sarcastic voice,
not quite sure why
I was being mean,
when this present wasn't
entirely
uncool.
The smile shattered and
fell from her face, piece by piece.
Still, no one had consulted me
on what I wanted to do this summer.
Annie, Alice, and I were
going to get babysitting jobs and
spend our days by the pool,
saving our money
for college.
And now I had to go to Israel?

And sit on some
stupid tour bus the whole time?
I'd always been curious about Israel.
I mean,
when you live in a place
like this,
where
nothing ever happens,
where
no one else
is Jewish,
where
everyone thinks you're weird
        because you don't celebrate Christmas,
Israel,
a country that looks so different
        exotic
        wild,
and where
the boys are handsome
and Jewish
        therefore datable
        (according to Mom and Dad),
sounds pretty good.

§ § §

But why couldn't they ask me before
making any plans?
I thought
you'd be happy, my mom said
in a tiny
voice.
I'm sorry, Mom. It's just that
Annie, Alice, and I had plans.
But this is great.
Really. I tried to make it better.
She began to look less sad.
Look, there are all kinds of trips you can
take, Sarah. There are hikes,
and you can take a bus all
over and see the whole country, she told me.
That's exactly what I don't want, Mom.
I want to do something different,
I said.
Okay . . . of course, different. It's you.
I should have known, nothing normal,
she muttered.
"Of course"
that dig had to come.
Well, look at this one, Sar, she said.

You could work on a kibbutz.
She pulled out one of the pamphlets
advertising for volunteers
for the communal farms.
I'd be working the land
like the first pioneers who built
the country out of nothing.
The photos on the glossy pamphlet
showed tan, smiling people
pulling apples down from trees,
sunning themselves by a swimming pool.
This looks sort of fun, I said.
The kibbutz? she asked.
I nodded my head, and she came
to stand beside me, resting
her hand on my arm.
You'll never be the same
after this trip, Sarah, she said.
It will change everything.
Mmm-hmm, I mumbled,
then returned to the chaos of
lines and planes,
my math homework.

      We'll see about that.

THE BAGGAGE CLAIM

Impatient people jostle each other
as they wait
for their suitcases to come
round on the carousel.
Women in babushkas and old
men in tattered jackets,
families of eight and ten.
Posters of palm trees
staring down from the wall
and teenagers with cell phones and Levi's
greeting me
as I enter
the five-thousand-year-old homeland
of the Jews.

Pushing and shouting and crowding and arguing.
Unaware of, indifferent to, my wonder.
I elbow my way to the front of the crowd
hovering in front of one carousel.

An elderly man stands next to me,
his hands in his pockets.
As a battered brown leather suitcase swings lazily
   into view,
the old man reaches over to pull it down.
As he reaches to pull the suitcase down,
his shirtsleeve inches up his arm.
As his shirtsleeve slides up,
I can make out
six green numbers etched neatly in a row
on his arm.
In his arm.
Indelible numbers,
history's reminder of one black mark
that can never be
erased.
I've never seen a Holocaust survivor before.
      Photographs of skeletal bodies
         empty eyes and striped pajamas
         a monstrous pile of shoes in a museum
         books lining the shelves
         in my parents' living room
         all those pictures and stories
         branded into my mind
            because We Mustn't Ever Forget.

But here's a living person.
He could have been in one of those photos,
could have lost his shoes to the Nazis.
His eyes aren't vacant.
Filled with life? Grandchildren?
Israel?

My suitcase, oversized, overstuffed,
and too heavy,
rounds the corner, tipping
dangerously.
I struggle to pull it
off the carousel but am unable.
The man with the numbers on his arm
gently nudges me away
and reaches for my suitcase.
Again those numbers
flash before my eyes,
and he hands me the handle
of my luggage.
I stammer a thank-you
and I walk away, suitcase rolling
behind me.

THE FIRST REUNION

The crowd here throbs with reunions,
embraces, tears.
A young man in a khaki soldier's uniform
kisses a woman passionately, while
gently wresting the handle of a suitcase
from her grasp.
Six Hasidic children play tag, as their
parents greet, with jovial hugs,
an old, wrinkled woman
who is tiny and
bent with age.
Sarah? a woman's voice shrills
across the hall.
A petite blonde runs towards me,
waving her arm at a dark bear of a man
who hesitates
several paces
behind her.
Michal? I ask.

She is my mother's second cousin.

My great-grandmother and her sister,

Michal's grandmother,

the only two of their family

who fled

and escaped

the pogroms

of the Cossacks

in Russia.

With the unspoken consent of the Russian czar,

the Cossacks attacked,

robbed,

and in the dead of night,

perpetrated whispered-of

   rapesmurderslootings.

So my great-great-grandparents began plotting

how they would send their children away.

Only two made it out.

Both sought refuge:

one in the land of the free and

home of the brave,

the other in the desert wilderness of her own people.

My matriarchal legacy.

§   §   §

Michal wraps me in
an embrace,
warm and welcoming.
Her perfume smells of wisteria and honey,
her hair of oranges.
She grins and spreads her arms wide,
holding me away from her.
You look just like your mother, she says.
Her yellow hair, brown eyes
look like my mother,
too.
And that's comforting.

ARRIVAL

The dusty parking lot
and dusty men are standing around outside
the arrivals hall, hawking their taxis
back to the city.
Cigarette smoke trails from their
tobacco-stained fingers.
Muddy vans and sedans lined up,
sitting in the late morning sunlight,
waiting for a ride while
concrete and heat linger
in the smells of a dry, crackly day.
This is it. I'm here.
The Middle East.
And it looks strange,
the men dark, their cars shabby
in a desert way.

Avi, Michal's husband,
drags my overstuffed suitcase

behind him.

It teeters on unsteady wheels.

You brought a lot of things with you,

Avi grunts softly.

Heat creeps up my neck.

I want—I need to become lean.

REMEMBERING, PART 2

Hey, Tubby. Nice uniform.
Stephanie eyed my clunkiness,
                 not so much fat, but
        starched jacket and pants
        in heavy polyester and wool
        gold epaulets and buttons
            too shiny
venom spitting from her
baby-blue eyes.
Looking it all up and down,
a wicked smirk
twisted her tanned
face,
while Jake stood there and
watched
in silence,
a witness.
She laughed

and looked at him
until he smiled,
too.
Coward.
Then she bouncedflounced away,
Jake in tow.
I took a tray from the stack
and made my way into the
hot food line,
my eyes rolling to keep
back the tears,
my stomach rolling, too.
Did anyone else hear her?
She was never that mean
before.
Usually they just ignored me.
I stood in the lunch line
trying to erase the
red marks her
words and
burning gaze, her
mocking grin
left.
My body twitching and itching

underneath the vilified
marching band uniform.
                    Pork chops for lunch.
Why.
Why the one day I didn't pack my lunch,
the one food that I couldn't eat?
Why.
Why today?
I told the lunch lady
with the pink hairnet
to save the pork chop
for someone else.
I don't want any.
But she spooned it up and
launched it onto my tray
anyway.
She grinned,
a nasty grin,
hollow eyes like a skull.
Some vegetables, Sugar?
Yes, please, I whispered.
Limp, grayish green beans
and browning carrots
swimming in an oil bubbly
buttery sauce.

Or something.
My stomach, still roiling
and reeling
from Stephanie's blow,
lurched anew.
And the tears were still there,
threatening.
I carried the tray carefully,
not wanting the meat
to touch the vegetables.
When I sat down heavily,
Annie and Alice,
munching on
white bread ham and cheese
sandwiches,
looked up startled.
What? I snapped.
I never spoke so sharply to them.
Their gentle cow eyes,
grazing over my tray,
across my face,
blanched hurt, and I
immediately felt guilty.
          Oh, joy,
                    Jewish guilt.

I'm sorry. I tried to make it better.
It's just that I can't eat this lunch,
and I'm starving, and . . .
And I couldn't bring myself
to tell my best,
my only
friends
what Stephanie had said
to me.
Why can't you eat your lunch?
Alice asked, voice
and eyes
brimming with innocence.
Because it's pork, I tell her.
So? A blank look.
So? I keep kosher, remember?
I can't eat pork.
Couldn't she remember anything?
But, Sarah, if you're hungry,
just eat it. What's the big deal?
Jeez,
Alice, I can't just
eat it
because I'm hungry.
It's against my religion,

remember?
I watched as Alice's mouth
flapped open and closed
as though she was trying
to formulate her apology or
shock or something,
and Annie's mouth
just hung agape.
I didn't want to hear it,
apologies, accusations,
none of it.
I threw my fork to the table,
threw my chair back,
stood up, and marched
        how fitting, in my uniform and all
out of the cafeteria.
        Maybe Fatty decided to start a diet,
I heard Stephanie snort
to the cheerleader hooligans.
I fled before their
laughter could reach me.
Outside, in the parking lot,
I bent down between
someone's Honda and
a pickup truck.

I coughed and choked,
not going to let myself cry.
But I was sick,
so sick.
Even between my best friends and me,
a breach.
I couldn't make it through
another two years
of high school.

ON THE ROAD AGAIN

Avi and Michal drive a small, white Fiat.
Looks like every other car on the road.
Small and white and covered
with a thin layer of grime.
Traffic moves quickly,
and cars
    dart in
                    and out
           of lanes.
Horns blare, men shout.
As a pickup truck swerves
in front of us,
Avi slams his hand down
on the steering wheel,
cursing in protest.
Michal turns to look at me.
She smiles joylessly.
It's not like Pennsylvania, eh, Sarah?

No, I shake my head.

It sure isn't.

None of the quiet politeness,

civility, concern for safety,

for life

that drivers have in my tiny hometown.

The scenery isn't as I pictured

in my mind.

Sand and scrubby cactus

low to the ground.

Dirt.

An occasional town of

cube-shaped, whitewashed

houses with red tile roofs

whizzes past.

Not the majestic desert dunes

I'd imagined.

This land, the buildings,

it all seems so scruffy

and low and

poor.

Not what I'd expected at all.

Still, as we drive on,

I can't help but feel

amazed,

attached,

bewildered.

Everyone in those cars,

in the garbage trucks

and the delivery vans,

they're Jewish.

Like me.

And as we drive on,

sand and trees and dull buildings

blur

my eyes.

The yellow yellow yellow . . .

REMEMBERING, PART 3

Spinning blonde pinwheeling blonde
on blonde
cheerleader curls
crashed into smashed into
those movie star looks
of his.

Stephanie cheered in her little red-and-white skirt
and the matching (tight) sweater.
And there I was, in that clunky, chunky red
marching band jacket,
clarinet resting on my lap.
She stood by the sidelines,
kicking up her legs,
and her pretty blonde curls
swished this way and that.

While I sat in my nerdy
polyesterandwoolblendedhideousuniform of a THING,

there he was, resting so easily on the bench
in his own red-and-white uniform,
clinging like skin to his form.

Why can't he see me?
      No one can see me.

If only he,
the most popular,
the most handsome
boy in school,
could see me.
He *should* see me.
But he saw what he wanted
to see,
what he needed to see.

We sat next to each other in math class,
trigonometry, to be exact.
Sometimes I could feel his eyes traveling
over and across the expanse of aisle,
taking me in,
wandering,
      crawling down
and caressing

the notebook open on my desk.

Once upon a time there was a big nerd
who Jake the Hottie only saw
when he looked at her
~~chest~~
I mean test
and copied the answers he spied there.
I knew it wasn't right.
That wasn't me.
I shouldn't want some jock jerk
like Jake.
But I did.
What's wrong with me?

And there he was after class,
walking too slowly towards the door,
glancing back over his shoulder at
      me?
Shifting his backpack while I packed mine,
already stuffed with books and
notebooks and pencils.
Hovering by the door.
Waiting?

I couldn't dillydally any longer, and so
I walked, on shaking legs, towards him.

He leaned in, whispering my name,
Sarah . . .
Conspiratorially.
           Ashamedly.
I, uh, can you, uh,
hardly the eloquence of expression
I'd imagined.
Can you, uh,
help me, uh,
with math?
I mean, help me study for it?
I stood there, my mouth hanging open,
struck dumb.
        dumb dumb dumb dumb dumb
Uh, sure.
Get a hold of yourself, Sarah.
He wanted me.
Me. To help. Him.
Do you want to come over tonight to study?
My sweetest, sultriest voice.
As if the second clarinet player in the

high school marching band could be sultry!
Maybe around eight o'clock?

Okay, he replied. Looking relieved.

Could it be, could he like me?
Why ask me . . . why not
Bill Wong or Audrey Timber
or stupid Stephanie?

That evening I gulped down two bites
of my mother's kosher meatloaf.
        All I could manage.
Then I ducked into my closet,
tearing through,
scrabbling, grappling through
the pants and skirts
and shirts hanging on their hangers.
I hadn't thought this hard about what to wear
ever.

A lavender skirt, white blouse;
a lavender sweater, blue jeans?
Settling on the lavender sweater,
        which really brought out my eyes,

and jeans, I set to fixing
my hair, my lip gloss.
Never tried this hard before.

I raced downstairs.
Seven o'clock.
Grabbed the log of cookie dough from the
refrigerator
and cut it up into tiny bits,
spooning it onto a cookie tray.
Jake would have warm cookies.

Did Stephanie bake for him?

The brass door knocker shaped like a dolphin
shuddered and boomed throughout the house.
I ran to get it, but my father got there first.
Dad, please! Please,
please, go away!
Oh it's a boy, huh? he smirked.
I just knew Jake heard him through the door.
I could die of embarrassment.

Jake and I set our books down on the
(freshly dusted) coffee table

in the living room.

Would you like some cookies?

My sweetest, sugar-coated voice

      because that's what boys like, right?

Uh, sure.

Arranged neatly on a plate,

pretty as can be,

but Jake didn't notice.

He simply snatched, shoveled, swallowed.

Well, should we start with chapter four? he asked.

So we got into it.

Three chapters.

Xs and Ys and *pi*'s.

But no conversation.

No soul-searching gazes.

No kisses.

And as soon as we were done,

he whispered a gruff word of thanks

and was on his way.

Then I was left alone,

picking up my books,

tossing the scrap paper,
wiping up his cookie crumbs.
And as I wiped up my tears,
I knew: It would always be this way.

NEARING JERUSALEM

The yellow is gone.
Changed to green.
No more dust sand sun.
The road climbs uphill,
and pine trees spring from the ground,
clawing their way towards the sky.
Green and gray rock.

     It's lovely here.
The road narrows,
and the car shudders with effort
as it clings to the concrete,
straining, pushing.
A red, rusty skeleton of an old truck
rests next to the highway.
Another in the grassy median.
And another, then another.
A monument to
this country's violent history.
A graveyard's peace shattered by the roar of traffic.

§ § §

My grandfather, who knew
so much persecution,
loved to tell me
stories of Jewish heroes.
From the Chanukah story
of the Maccabee warriors
defeating Greek invaders
to the Jewish fighters who drove tin trucks
carrying food and water
to a starved, thirsty Jerusalem
under the watchful eye
of the sniper's rifle
during Israel's war of independence.
These trucks now strewn alongside the road,
a reminder of the bravery of those
who pressed and
sometimes died
for Israel's bloody birth.
I heard of them in stories.
But here,
between
the faces of the mountains,
they slumber on.

§ § §

My grandfather was so proud of
"Our Boys,"
the Israeli soldiers
who fought and were strong.
And I was so proud,
to think that maybe I, too,
didn't have to be
just one of those Smart Jews.
I could be strong and brave, too,
a hero.

Michal turns around again.
We're near Jerusalem now.
Here we go.

A NEW WORLD

Perfect.
A shady nook with pale stone walls
the color of flesh.
I sit on the balcony with a glass of orange juice
in my hand.
Rosemary crawls over the lip
of a wooden planter
in shades of indigo and sage.
I inhale the heady scent of the jasmine
blossoms, so delicate in their whiteness.
The smell sits on top of the air, smothers it.
Pungent but wonderful.
I could get lost in it, I think.
And this is when I know
I have been transported
to another place, exotic
and not altogether safe.
A quiet mixes with the fragrance.
There are car engines and buses far off,

but my space, here, is filled with my own silence.
I could sit here and feel I am alone
and okay.

And it occurs to me
that there are so many things
I can do.
Things I don't have to do.
There is a life beyond what my parents
and high school have
prescribed for me.
There are new languages and countries
and jasmine blossoms inviting me
to go,
to keep searching.
So many emotions
        passion love excitement
to let in.
But first, I need to strip down
and get rid
of all the baggage.
That of marching band geeks and nerds.
Who never have boyfriends or French kisses.
Whose parents and teachers and
friends and enemies

expect and expect of them,
and fill the hazy
outlines of a body
with only what they want to see.
The excess luggage of the invisible ones.
My mom says those people
have the most fun when they're older.
         I want it now.
So I will work and explore
and be by myself
and eventually the trappings
will fall away.
I will emerge,
naked and shorn of
all the noise of
everyone else's voices.
Then everyone will see.
Me.

The buildings here on this street
all look the same.
Slightly decayed.
At the end of their better days.
Yet sandy and elegant.
Tall cedar trees

sway gently and shade balconies that
face the street.
The noise of pots and pans banging,
voices raised, laughter,
human sounds
rings out.
This city breathes, and I can feel its heart beat.
I've only just arrived, I know, but I am part of this
    humming,
this living.
And there has been life here for so long.
Jewish life.
Life that nursed me and cursed me,
leaving me marked in school.
The Jew.
Every fall,
when the other kids are
warming up for
football practice or field hockey,
I'm in a dress sitting next to my parents
in the synagogue
for those alien Jewish holidays.
Moss green seats upholstered in crushed velveteen,
the rabbi in his white robe at the front,

the antique Torah scrolls with their elaborate
silver crowns.
There, the history,
God,
doesn't feel real or close.
But here it all does.
And I'm only sitting on someone's balcony
watching the trees
and smelling the flowers.

Behind me, inside, I hear the sounds of scuffling,
echoing the crashing and voices
from the other apartments.
A door opens and slams shut.
Squeals of joy. Michal's laughter.
Her boys,
the soldiers,
are home.
I rise and go in to meet
my heroic Israeli cousins.

THE BOYS

They have arrived, tall and
copper with sun.
Like sand gods in olive khakis
and scuffed black boots.
Bulging backpacks and their guns
long and not altogether real-looking,
like they belong to a movie set
in Hollywood.
The boys are home from the army.

But there are three of them.
I recognize two from the photos,
Natan and Assaf,
     my cousins,
but the third is not familiar.
A stranger.

Dark brown eyes
and hints of golden light.

He is long and thin and much
older looking.

I can hardly see my cousins.
I know I should want to meet them,
but I can't focus,
because my eyes are fastened on his.

My stomach tightens.
I can hardly breathe.
And he's staring right back at me.
What does he see?
What could he possibly see?
A band geek?
Even though he doesn't know.
But maybe my mother told Michal
who told her sons
who told him?
Our cousin, the dork from the States is coming to visit....
But maybe he simply sees
a girl.

Does he know what I'm thinking?
Can he see it on my face?
In my eyes?

Michal's voice comes back to me.
She's introducing me to my cousins,
Natan, who is short and hairy
like his father,
bowlegged and sturdy and dark,
and Assaf, who is tall and lean,
with hair the golden color of wheat
and green eyes much like my own.
She pauses, smiling, proud.
Then her hand flies to her mouth.
A gesture of embarrassment.
Oh, I forgot!
This is Lior, Assaf's friend
from the army,
she explains.
Now that I should look at him,
I can hardly force my eyes in his direction.
I nod my head and look at the floor.
I can feel the crimson heat of a blush tiptoeing
over my shoulders and neck and cheeks.
I glance at him quickly and he is smiling at me,
an unintelligible expression playing at his
pink lovely lips,
almost as if he is laughing at me.
Natan and Assaf are not interested

in me
as they turn this way and that,
looking for a convenient place to drop
their bags and guns.
Michal, a mother hen
cooing and clucking and fretting,
fusses over them
then announces that dinner is ready,
first in Hebrew, then,
turning to me, in English.
Michal carries a pair
of brass candlestick holders to the table
and motions for me to stand next to her.
She pulls a delicate lace shawl
over her head and lights the candles.
She places her hands
over her eyes,
covering them,
and whispers a prayer.
I watch her, transfixed.
With her eyes closed, she passes her hands
over the flames
three times,
softly singing under her breath.
A mystical scene.

§   §   §

Then the three boys—
　　　though it feels wrong to call them boys,
　　　having seen the large rifles that they carry
and Avi come to the table,
talking noisily in Hebrew.
My heart or my stomach or something inside
is fluttering a mile a minute,
and I'm afraid I won't be able to eat.
Avi picks up the kiddush cup
　　　the ceremonial goblet
　　　for the blessing over the wine
and quickly says a prayer,
then the blessing over the challah bread.
It's funny,
it's a prayer I've heard before
when my father recites it at our own holiday meals,
but it sounds so foreign, so different here.
And it strikes me that the Hebrew we say
only in our prayers
is their everyday language.
And Avi—the others—their Hebrew
sounds so different
from our awkward American fumbling
over the ancient letters.

So fluid and fast.

Words running into words so I can't distinguish.

Not that I'd understand anyway.

The table is overflowing with platters,

lamb and chicken

and salads of diced tomatoes and olives,

peppers and beets, more meat,

and in the center, a vase

of brilliant red

gladiolas.

Everyone is reaching for the food,

hungrily, greedily.

They're talking fast and loud in Hebrew

that Michal sometimes remembers

to translate for me,

but I couldn't care or concentrate

     anyway.

All I want is to run outside onto the balcony

and to catch my breath.

     And for Lior to follow me.

The smell of chicken stewed with tomatoes

sends me back to my parents' yellow

kitchen with wooden cabinets

and white flowered curtains.

The memory is so strong,
I forget
where I am, that I am no longer
a child
in my parents' home.
Then I glance up from my plate
across the table
at Lior and remember.
No, I'm not a child
any longer.
And every time
I look at him,
I am surprised to see that Lior
        could it be?
is watching me.
And other times when I lift
my eyes off my plate
to see what the others are doing or saying,
I catch Michal
studying both of her sons' faces carefully,
as though searching for signs of harm
that they suffered in their absence
but would never speak of.
A crease forms between her eyes, below the forehead,

and a flicker of something
         sadness, maybe?
passes over her brow.

I rise to help her clean up
after the meal is finished
and the boys, or men,
have left the table.
As I pass her sudsy dishes
to rinse,
she asks me about my mother.
I tell her she's fine, and Michal
remarks,
catching me by surprise,
how different their lives must be.
My mother,
never having to worry about
an army taking her child
away.
I reply, though
maybe I shouldn't,
that she worries
anyway.
She worries I will be killed

each time I get into a car with my friends.
And then I realize,
Michal's fears
are no joke, and I
inspect her face and notice
how deep are the lines
etched in her forehead
and around her eyes.
She looks so weary.
And I ask, though
maybe I shouldn't,
Aren't you proud of them, fighting for Israel?
She glances at me, the lines deepen,
her mouth screwed up in a grimace.
Yes, I'm proud of them, Sarah,
but not for fighting.

THE BALCONY SCENE

We say our good nights and
I go to bed.
I intend to go to sleep,
and I change into my pajamas.
But I know it's a lost cause.
And sure enough,
turning and churning,
so jumpy and fidgety,
twisting the sheets around myself.
I crawl out of bed, groping for the light switch.
I ease out of my room
and into the living room,
open the balcony door, and
instantly feel a rush of relief
as the cool, perfumed air
envelops me and makes me feel calmer.
I sit in the round cushiony chair and look out
at the dark silhouettes of the trees and
other houses.

I imagine what my parents are doing now.

They must be coming home from work.

Maybe it's still too early for that, though.

It's strange to think that they

are almost a third of a day

behind me.

A new day will begin for me

as they are still fast asleep in their beds.

I wonder if they're thinking about me,

if they miss me.

I can't sort out how I feel.

I miss the way my mom smells,

of apple dish soap and lilacs

all at once.

And I miss how safe

that smell made me feel.

The comfort I used to find

leaning my cheek

against the scratchy cushion

of my dad's beard.

But this is exciting,

the kind of adventure I've always hoped for,

never really believed possible.

For me.

I wonder what the other kids from my class

are doing this summer.
Probably most of them
are hanging around town.
My mind is dancing all around, and
when it touches on Lior, I get that weak
sillyslidey feeling inside.
I wonder what he thinks of me.
Is he thinking of me?
At school, most of the other kids
        especially boys
don't seem to find me
remarkable enough to consider.
Or even remember.
But I thought he was looking at me during dinner.
        Probably my imagination.
I wonder if he has a girlfriend.
Maybe she's a soldier, too.
I wonder what it's like to be in the army.
Assaf and Lior are only two years older
than I am.
I can't imagine feeling much older
in two years.
Old enough to carry a gun.
Or to use it.
Assaf and Lior are in the elite paratroopers unit.

They are combat soldiers.
They have to fight.
Possibly kill.
And though part of me
wishes that I could fight,
that I could be strong, too,
I feel sad for them.
Poor Lior, with those warm, brown eyes.
I wonder how he grew up knowing this
is what he would have to do.
Have to be.
Or maybe growing up
with the violence, the fear
made him *want* to be a soldier someday.
        Today.

Suddenly, the sliding glass door rumbles open.
I am startled out of my thoughts.
I spin around.
I know it will be him.
I hope it will be him.
Then he is beside me.
Mind if I sit with you? Lior asks.
He is smiling, hair standing up at odd angles.

He is wearing a white cotton T-shirt and
rumpled shorts.
It looks like he was tossing around in bed, too.
My stomach is in knots,
my own wrinkled T-shirt,
oversized,
inherited from my father,
and gym shorts
embarrassing me.
But his eyes look kind.
And there's something else there,
something fiery and intense.
I'm not used to boys looking at me
      like this.
Sure, not at all.
I slide my chair over a bit so he can settle
into the one next to mine.
He sits down and stares out into the darkness.
We don't speak.
I can hardly sit still,
so keenly aware of his presence,
a dark silhouette,
a rich cinnamon smell.
His voice suddenly interrupts the silence.

From where are you in America?
His accent is funny.
The words are all there
but the order mixed up.
And he says his *r*'s funny, too,
like they're lodged in the back
of his throat.
But it's the first time all night
someone has asked me a question
about myself.
Pennsylvania. Not so far
from Philadelphia, I answer.
I've never been to Philadelphia.
Only to New York, he says.
Oh.
I try desperately to think of how to
keep the conversation
going.
Where are you from in Israel?
A small village in the north,
near Lebanon.
He pauses.
Why did you come here?
he asks me.
I'm startled.

It's such an abrupt question
and I'm not sure how to answer.
I'm going to volunteer on a kibbutz,
I respond.
Which one?
Kfar Avivim, I tell him.
That is close to my village. I know it.
He pauses.
But why Israel?
There is a lull.
I cannot think of how to answer.
He's going to think I'm stupid and can't
carry on a conversation.
We sit facing straight ahead,
still not looking at one another.
I turn to him.
He is smiling.
The moonlight is reflecting off his face,
casting a silvery halo about him,
streaking through his hair.
I don't know.
Because I'm Jewish, and Israel is
supposed to be my homeland
I guess.
And my parents

thought I should come.
But they won't leave me alone.
About school, what colleges I'll apply to,
everything.
I stop.
Why am I telling him this?
It must seem so unfair to him
that these are my problems,
      trivial,
while he has to think about staying alive.
Or killing people.
I say so to him.
It's okay. You are lucky,
he says.
We lose so much time in the army, three years.
He brings his two forefingers to his lips,
meeting in a point.
But that's how it is.
Then he turns to me and
I can feel him studying my profile.
You're pretty, you know that?
No, I whisper.
My heart is beating like crazy.
No one

other than my parents
has ever said anything like this to me.
And it's him.
A boy.
      The boy?
Well, you are,
he murmurs.
I turn to look at him and he smiles.
Then he reaches across the arm of my chair
and takes my hand in his.
It's such a simple gesture.
But it is tender
and warm.
And we sit there in silence,
until the sun rises.

JERUSALEM

We try to keep from running out the door,
down the stairs,
into the morning sun.
But we can't get out fast enough, can't wait
to get away from the others,
to have the city all to ourselves.
A flicker of guilt,
     leaving my newfound family behind,
        darts across my chest, my mind
               but I brush it aside.
We race out onto the street, and he grabs my hand.
The road is quiet, no cars.
No buses or traffic on Shabbat, here.
Not like home, where everyone goes
to the mall on Saturdays.
The giant cedars sway in the gentlest of breezes,
but I still feel the first drops of sweat trickling
down my temples, collecting over my lip.
Lior looks so cool.

Gun slung over his shoulder,
he's wearing mirrored sunglasses,
and I can't see his eyes.
Maybe it's better that way,
because I am struck speechless
        every time he catches my gaze.
Walking next to him, I feel
all too aware of his long body.
My shoulder rubbing against his arm.
Who am I?
Who is this girl I thought I knew
standing beside this tall, strong man
who is dark and strange to me?
The girl I used to recognize
never walked alongside a man
        other than her father.
I never walked as one half of a couple.
I feel like a fraud.
But Lior and I walk hand in hand.
We don't speak.
Then his sure grip on my hand reminds me.
Those long, slender, olive-colored fingers,
they are laced with *mine*.
And they're beautiful.

§　§　§

The street is shady, and Lior leads me
to the right, around a bend
a short distance away,
and we come to a café, where I can
hear the sounds of plates banging and
people laughing.
We enter a shady courtyard off the sidewalk
filled with fat palm trees,
garish cobalt-blue tables and chairs,
and the smell of eggs and vegetables and frying oil.
We sit down at one of the tables,
Lior resting his rifle between his knees,
and he speaks to the waiter in Hebrew.
I don't know what he says,
but then the waiter returns with menus.
Lior hands one to me and I look at it,
then my heart drops.
It's in Hebrew.

      I can't read it.
Lior looks up and understands my expression.
I'll translate for you.
He smiles, pushing his sunglasses to rest
on top of his head.
Oh, those brown eyes
with the golden flecks,

I could look into them for hours.
And black curls lining his forehead,
like a dusty Caesar.
He reads the menu to me.
There are all kinds of juices,
orange, strawberry, apple, pear,
and there are salads,
Israeli, with diced cucumbers and tomatoes,
or Greek, with olives and feta.
Everything is soaked in olive oil.
There is chicken liver, eggplant sandwiches,
cheese, pumpkin soup.

But who eats soup in this heat? I wonder.
I order a fruit salad dressed in honey
and strawberry juice,
and Lior orders eggs.
He eats quickly, like a wolf,
throwing the food into his mouth
as fast as he can.
When he catches me watching him,
he looks abashed and grins.
Sorry, I am used to the army. We only
get seven minutes to eat.
I smile back at him.
Don't worry.

He has cleared his plate and I've
barely touched mine.
You eat slow,
he says,
but I can help you.
We both laugh.
Then I start to shovel
the fruit into my mouth, too.
I feel self-conscious.
I've never liked eating in front of strangers.
With a boy I like across the table
it's even worse.
But he's sweet,
and he starts to stack the sugar packets
into a pyramid
so he's not staring at me.
It rises quite high.
I'm done, I tell him.
Okay, so let's get the bill and go.
He turns to look for the waiter
and shouts something at him.
I guess he asked for the check.
Does he think I'm stupid, because I
don't understand?

Is he getting frustrated with me?
But he doesn't question me or comment.
And I am relieved.
We leave the blue tables behind
and head back to the street.
We continue to walk through my cousins'
neighborhood, Rehavia.
The spicy aroma of the jasmine
fills the air, fills me.
Creeping vines slip over the buildings,
which are crumbling
and aged,
covered with the grime and soot of millennia.
Yet they are graceful and stately,
built with the same stone.
The Jerusalem stone
that sometimes gleams
a pale gold, other times it is
blanched almost white.
As we move towards the center of the city,
the buildings grow increasingly decrepit.
Crookedly roosting on top of each other,
shuttered windows peeking out
like hens stacked in a henhouse.

The streets wind around
　　　and
double back
　　　on each other.
They make no sense.
More ungainly, golden buildings,
now varnished a powdery black,
with signs I cannot read.
But Hebrew is my language, nonetheless.
The language of my prayers,
Lior's language.
I cannot explain it to myself.
I love this city, the sleepiness, the peace.
It's not
what I expected Jerusalem to be,
with the news always broadcasting the horrors
of bombs and death.
But here it is,
an exquisite tangle of life.
The most beautiful spot I've ever seen.

WALTZING AWAY

And as we continue our stroll,
our waltz
through the city,
it occurs to me
that I never dreamed I would
be in the Middle East.
I never thought that I would
make it out of Pennsylvania.
But really, I had hoped
I'd get away.
Someday.
Out and away from Stephanie
and her cheerleading gang
with their little skirts and poofy blonde hair
and the fools
who set so much store by them.
Where even my friends
stand across an uncrossable gulf,
a strait of murky waters

and ideas of heaven and hell
and who's going where
yawning between us.
Our gods poised on opposite
shores.
And where religion is
a conscious decision
every day of my
life.

I dreamed of escaping school dances
where the boys
and girls
stand around
uncomfortably
on opposite sides
of the gymnasium,
peering at each other
suspiciously
like enemies on opposing sides
of the battlefield.
Looking longingly
with hope
or scorn,

sometimes with disappointment.
And no one ever asking me to dance.

But I bet Lior would ask me to dance.
I imagine slow dancing with him,
his rifle slung over his shoulder,
bumping against us as we sway to the music,
his arms around my waist,
my hands clasped behind his neck.

(The stance never varies at the dances.)
But the gun,
that would make
for an interesting change.
I still can't comprehend
how casually he carries the rifle,
so natural it seems to be,
like it is a piece of his anatomy.
He should be as much a child as I still am.
But he looks old.
Really old.

THE OLD CITY

The high walls of the Old City rise up before us.
Palm trees, silent sentinels,
stand in a snaking line around the walls,
which are also made of the Jerusalem stone.
An arched portal, the Jaffa Gate,
tall, dark, and menacing, with graffiti
in Arabic and Hebrew sprayed
on the massive blocks,
welcomes us as we enter the Old City.

I smell it before I see it.
Corn on the cob grilling over open fires.
Arab men, grimy from the smoke, stand
over the flames.
A plaza jammed
with taxis and street vendors,
trinkets and souvenirs
hanging in the windows of the rundown stores.

Passing through the cavelike entryway
of Jaffa Gate
is like hopping back through the centuries.
Here I can see the Arab market,
a lightless, narrow lane,
but I can't see far.
My stomach begins to clench.
Michal said
I'm not supposed to go there.
An unnamed threat.
Lior leads me past, still holding fast to my hand,
rifle swinging.
We pass through a cavernous
alleyway, and all around I can hear the sounds of
praying and singing and thumping,
almost as if hundreds of people
are banging on their tables
out of time with one another.
They're Jewish.
The Jews live right on top of the Arabs here.
I never guessed.
I expected—I don't know.
Distance.
But there's no space.

And Shabbat is out in full force here.
The throbbing sounds of
my Jewish Sabbath.

The alleyway is lined
with old, beige stone houses
piled on top of one another,
crammed one next to the other,
with carved, arched windows and doors.
Through the open windows,
tables and people and shelves of books are visible.
It's amazing.
My Shabbat.
Saturday,
not Sunday like my friends' Sabbath.
My holiday,
    and here it's normal.

Everything smells different.
The air is laced with spices and cooking and dirt.
The scent of a foreign life.
Do you want to go to the Kotel? Lior asks.
Where?
I'm confused.
And frustrated.

Why don't I understand Hebrew?
I studied it for ten years
three days a week after school.
When all the other girls were in
Girl Scout meetings,
I had to go to Hebrew school.
A lot of good it did me.
The Kotel, the Western Wall.
I can feel his stare, piercing through the sunglasses.
I know I'm blushing.
Oh. Yes, I'd like to go there. Please,
I stammer.
The holiest place on earth for Jews.
The last remnant of the Holy Temple.
Jews all over the world face
in the direction of the Wall as they pray.
He nods and chuckles
then pulls me along.
His strides are so long, I'm practically skipping
to keep up with him,
trying to keep from sliding on
the worn, slippery cobblestones.
We come to a wider tunnel, cavernous and dank.
There is a checkpoint
with a metal detector ahead.

Five religious Jews
in their black hats and frock coats,
long beards,
are waiting to pass.
An older Arab couple
       the man wearing a ratty brown suit,
       a black-and-white checked headdress,
       and thick, Coke-bottle glasses,
       and the woman in a scratchy-looking gray
       robe, with a black silk scarf
       covering her head,
stand ahead of us.
As the Jewish men pass through
the security check with ease,
the Israeli soldiers manning the
metal detector
bark at the Arab couple and
wave them forward.
I notice the man and woman exchange a glance
before stepping up to the security gate.
One soldier checks their identity
cards, as another
rifles through the woman's purse,
before dumping the contents

onto a table and
pawing through her belongings.
The soldiers talk loudly
and laugh,
gesturing towards the couple.
Something in my chest
constricts.
And I wonder how I got through
Hebrew school
        life
never realizing that in this land there were
old people and
normal people
who are just trying to walk
around
and go to their jobs,
that there is life here and
it isn't only what some people
want us to believe.
        That it's about
        God
        or bombs
        and violence.
        Jews and Arabs.

Right and Wrong.

Them and Us.

Black and White.

Then it's our turn.

Lior shows his I.D. card and I open my purse.

We're waved through.

And the ease of it

makes me feel

a little sick.

We step out into the sunlight.

I blink rapidly

while Lior pulls his glasses

back down

over his face.

I look to my left.

There's the Wall.

Not quite as I'd imagined it.

There's so much space.

A large, open plaza spreads out in front of the Wall,

and there are policemen

standing on guard

along the sides.

With their guns.

What an odd mix, religion and rifles.

A high partition divides the large men's side
from the smaller women's section.
Somehow, I thought it would feel closer, warmer.
I thought I'd feel nearer to God here.
There's more space than I was prepared for.
And the sea of black hats, swaying and bowing,
alienates me.
I'm not a part of their world.
Yet, as bizarre as the people under those black hats
look to me,
I envy their unquestioning bonds.
They know their world.
For it is so close
and uncompromising and
tight.
I'm Jewish, too, but I'm different.
That unquestioning sense of
faith,
        I don't have it.
How do I feel about God?
I think He exists . . .
but there is no one to
show me the way to believe.
There is nothing in my world

to let me feel sure
and safe
in my beliefs.

As I peer closely,
I can see that there are
soldiers praying at the Wall
and tourists with their cameras click-clacking away.
The Wall doesn't belong only to the black hats.
As we step into the plaza,
Lior stops.
I'll wait for you here.
You're not coming? I ask.
No, I don't pray here.
Why?
He looks away. *Go on,*
I'll wait for you.
I turn quickly
and walk towards the women's section of the Wall.
Suddenly it's breathtaking.
Immense sand-colored blocks stacked
one
on
top
of

the
other.
I can't even make
out the cracks in
between.
I stare up, but I can't see the top.
Some of the stones are bright
and seem new,
others are corroded and smooth
from the touch
of millions of hands.
The stained-glass windows
from our synagogue in Pennsylvania
flash into my mind,
blazing under my eyelids.
Carefully cut shards of pink and yellow
and orange glass
fit carefully together in no recognizable pattern.
Then, the stale, greenish upholstery
arranged in perfect rows
facing the outdated wooden podium for the rabbi.
Everything so artificial.
So planned and human.
But here, these wild blocks of stone
carved from the mountains

and molded from sand,

       their assembly a mystery.

A better tribute, I think.

I make my way through an untidy crowd of chairs

       like those found behind desks in a

       fourth-grade classroom

and women praying.

I sit on a chair and watch.

The woman next to me is softly weeping.

She is also praying.

I feel like I'm about to fall backwards.

A pigeon's head peeks out

from the scrubby brush

growing in the crack between two bricks.

He looks around, nonchalantly.

Who is the pigeon that gets to live

in the Western Wall?

I remember that I am supposed to write

a prayer on a piece of paper

and stick it into the Wall.

I tear a page from my notebook

and scribble a prayer

asking for my parents' health

and my own.

Should I ask for Lior to kiss me?
No, I think better of it.
I shouldn't be too selfish,
at the holiest place in the world.
I walk to the Wall,
place my hand on the stone in front of me.
It is cool.
I look for the crevice
where it meets its neighboring stone
and the crack is hardly the width of a slip of paper.
I have no words now
but there are tears just behind my eyes.
How did they ever build this?
I look straight up at the blue, blue sky.
Is God up there?
What is He thinking?
Do the people who come to the Wall to pray
get preferential treatment?
The woman standing at my side
is silently bobbing her head,
holding a prayer book right up to her face,
rubbing it over her nose.
Up and down, up and down.
The navy blue scarf covering her head
moves up and down,

keeping time with some rhythm in her mind.
I let my fingers crawl over the stone
into the crevices
looking for a niche for my note.
Every time I think I've found a spot
where my tiny, folded-up square of paper will fit,
twenty other prayers fall out
onto the ground.
What happens to someone who drops
other people's prayers
on the ground
at the holiest site on the planet?
I check to see if the woman in the navy headscarf
is watching me dislodge the other prayers.
What if one of them is hers?
Finally, I manage to wedge my prayer
into a crack
without displacing
more than a few other notes.
And as a wave of emotion
passes over me
again,
I wonder why.
I mean, my family isn't so religious.
We keep kosher

and go to synagogue two
times a year,
but I sense
for my parents it's more about
tradition than
spirituality
or faith.
And I guess I've
always felt the same way.
Maybe the power of this place
is in the size—
people, my people hauled
these stones for something great
that they believed in.
And generations of my people have
prayed here,
and I am keeping this giant tradition alive,
too, coming here.
It's all so mythical
and big.
And overwhelming.
I whisper the Sh'ma, the
only prayer I can remember

    Sh'ma Yisrael, Adonai Elohaynu, Adonai Echad.
    Hear O Israel, the Lord is God, the Lord is One.

I touch the wall and kiss my hand.
Then I turn away
and walk back to the plaza,
back to Lior.
Neither of us speaks, then
he takes my hand,
and I bid farewell to this most
holy spot
where God is always present.

KISSED

We're not touching now
as we make our way through
the snaking alleyways and
tunnels
of the Old City.
Just walking, next to each other.
Each staring straight ahead.
Suddenly, Lior stops and turns to me.
He pulls me into the shadows
at the side of the path and
silently he takes my hand and pushes
his sunglasses off his face.
The he leans down and kisses my mouth,
so gently, so sweetly.
His lips are salty.
My eyes are squeezed shut,
but I think he is watching me.
I open my eyes and see his are closed,

and he has this peaceful look on his brow.
I feel like I'm falling forward.
Then it's over.
Was that okay? he asks me.
It's not my first kiss,
but it's my first real one.
I don't think Mike Donner
from the marching band counts.
He had braces and a swollen trumpet lip
the time he kissed me
when I was storing my clarinet
in the instrument closet.
I don't know what to say.
I can't say anything.
My tongue feels glued fast to the back of my teeth.
He looks at me, wondering if I'm upset with him.
I smile and reach a shaking hand to his cheek.
It's rough and I pull it down to me again.
Then I kiss him.
I have never done that before.
We step back into the light
and find our way to the other side
of the walls
and retrace our steps

back to Michal's house.
Sharing kisses, and I am blushing
and still not believing I'm holding
this handsome Israeli soldier's hand.

GOOD-BYE

My cousins and Lior
leave at dusk.
A distant good-bye.
Hands and chins solemnly raised
in a wave and nod of leave-taking,
in that way that boys do it.
Lior kisses me again
and touches my cheek,
and quietly he shuts the door
behind him.
Lior is gone.
He didn't like to talk about the army.
He said that mostly it's just fun,
     fooling around with his friends,
     looking at the girl soldiers,
     and telling stupid jokes to pass the time.
But he won't tell me about the other stuff.
I can only imagine.
Or I can't.

I don't feel frightened,
        in danger
here.
But Lior has to carry his gun.
He has to.

He has left me with promises
of telephone calls and visits.
I gather my clothes,
a hairdryer,
books, and shoes
into my suitcase,
folded messily, and the zipper
hardly closes.
Too many things.
What do I need them for?
Just cluttering my brain,
space.
It's a mess.
Michal comes to my room
and says Avi will drive me to the bus station.
She sits on the bed and watches
as I, redfaced,
try to pull the zipper shut.
Life on kibbutz is very hard, she says

out of the blue.
But you will be all right.
Michal leans over
and presses down on the suitcase
so I can finally close it.
Thanks. Um, Michal, I ask,
will the food be kosher there?
Yes, she answers.
The food is kosher
pretty much everywhere here.
But you probably won't find
much religion on the kibbutz.
Kibbutzniks, well, most of them
seem to hate religion.
Judaism.
Why? I ask.
I am not sure. I think it has
to do with getting away
from the old ways.
The old European ways
that they see as weak.
I guess that makes sense,
I reply slowly.
What about Shabbat?
Will they celebrate it?

Nobody works on Shabbat
in Israel, Michal tells me.
But I doubt they will light
candles.
Oh, I mumble.
I am surprised, but
when I think about
how they fought for the land
and how the history,
at least the modern history,
of the
Jews seems filled with
weakness,
it doesn't seem so strange.
Suddenly, I feel embarrassed,
not having spent
any time with the family.
Michal, I begin,
I'm sorry I didn't . . .
I don't even know how to finish.
Nonsense, she answers.
This is what you should do
when you are in a new place.
You should have fun.
Anyway, we'll talk while

you are on the kibbutz,
so I can be your mother in Israel
and make sure everything is fine.
She is kind and I am
relieved.
She helps me lift the
suitcase off the bed,
and we return to the white Fiat.
It stutters and trembles
through the cramped streets,
and suddenly
Avi pulls to the side of the road.
Michal opens her door
and I get out, too.
We take my luggage down some steps,
and the bus station spreads below.
A plaza
         a parking lot
covered
with sand-colored canopies,
take-out falafel and pastry kiosks,
and ticket windows at the head of it all.
Soldiers with heavy canvas duffel bags,
youths with backpacks and
hiking boots, and old women

with scarves tied around their heads,
laden with plastic
shopping bags,
mill around.
Soldiers are
saying their good-byes
to girlfriends and lovers,
kissing,
peering deeply,
earnestly into
their eyes.
I think of Lior
and feel myself blushing.
The buses are parked in a long line,
and a short metal bench
slants in front of each of them.
Michal buys my ticket for me
and takes me to my row.
Do you want anything to eat? she asks.
No, thank you, I reply.
Once I am on the bus,
stifled and sweaty and hot,
I regret not buying a bottle of soda
or water. Anything
to quench the dryness in my throat,

the dryness in the air.
Most of the other passengers
are soldiers,
boys and girls.
They sit in pairs, talking loudly,
laughing often.
I wish I knew what they were joking about.
I wish I was one of them.
Israeli.
A soldier.
But then some of the male soldiers,
the ones I saw in the station
bidding their romances farewell,
now make crude gestures,
and I just know
that they are making fun of the
girls they kissed away.
And I can't help but wonder
if Lior is mocking me
in the same way.
I mean, I don't really know him.
Anything about him.
What books does he read?
Does he even like to read?
Music, movies?

I know nothing, except
he's Israeli, he's a soldier,
and he looks very handsome
in his olive uniform.
It's all so romantic.
I suppose.
The memory of our kisses
forces flutters
through my belly
and a smile to my lips.

HEADING NORTH

The bus creeps out of Jerusalem,
drives down the hills
I climbed two days earlier,
and the valley and the mountains
spread out beneath me,
and it feels like the bus will
take flight
as the driver accelerates.
Then we are driving
somewhere north
or west
of Jerusalem.
We're going
straight and straight,
passing through beat-up towns
marked by gas stations
and falafel stands.
And long stretches of sand
and tangled, brownish brush,

rocks, and it's all as dry as it gets.
A soldier sits across the aisle from me,
his rifle standing balanced between his knees.
He is holding an unlit cigarette
between his first and second fingers,
placing it between his lips, then
pulling it out and exhaling
        pantomiming a smoke.
We have entered the mountains,
brown and naked,
and to the east, a sapphire lake.
I can't stop looking at it.
The water is blue and opaque,
a lake like any I've seen on camping trips
in the mountains in the Poconos.
But I've never seen this Sea of Galilee before.
The Jews of old lived on its shores,
and Jesus walked across these waters.
History lives here.
And my ancient ancestors lived here.
So long ago,
I can only read about them in the Bible,
and I don't even know their names.
The lake seems to live and breathe,
as our hot, musty bus drives past,

and all the other cars on the highway race by.
The driver turns around and tells me my stop is next.
We pull up to a small town.
There is a gas station with a slanting
overhang shading the pumps.
I stand and grab my things and step off the bus.
The place is desolate.
I have a paper with directions in my pocket,
how to reach the kibbutz from town.
I cross the highway, timidly, then fast
and with my eyes closed
as cars and tankers bomb
down six lanes of roadway.
And straight ahead is another road,
smaller, lined by fields.
At the edge is a small concrete post
with a bench that looks like a bus stop.
But it's not.
It's a hitching post.
As in hitchhiking.
I am to stay there until a car
with the kibbutz name painted on the hood
passes.
Then I must flag it down and ask for a ride.

I've never hitchhiked.

Never.

And I've never wanted to.

My whole body is shaking.

My stomach is queasy.

I am scared out of my mind.

The letter also says not to get in an unmarked car,

because there is an Arab village nearby, and I shouldn't

get into a car with Arabs.

A lingering threat of

     I'm not even sure what.

I close my eyes against the burning sun.

The air is sweltering, and I can

hardly

draw

a

breath.

I imagine the junipers and rosebushes

lining the sidewalk

in front of my house

and the old dogwood tree at the side,

dripping snowy white blossoms.

I'm on my bike, and air
that is cool
and free of dust
blankets my face.
I coast down the hill
on the road to the creek,
past the creek to the mall,
and every tree, every house—even the cars—
looks familiar
and safe.
I hear the throb of an engine and
my eyes jerk open.
My heart jumps into my mouth.
I see a car about to turn onto the road.
It's white and small.
What do I do?
Should I stand up, flag it down?
Is the kibbutz name on it?
No, there's nothing.
I stay seated, and the car slows down
as it passes my post
but doesn't stop.
The back windows are framed
by heavy curtains,

black velvet
tied back with golden tassels.
An older couple ride in the front,
the man driving.
And two young Arab women
are in the back seat,
their heads covered by dark veils.
They turn to look at me as the car
drives by.
Eyes veiled, too.
They look so un-American
        not like me or anyone I've
        ever known.
But they're two girls riding
in the back of their
parents' car.
        Ordinary.
I wonder what they think
when they see me?
A Jew?
Someone who
they might automatically assume
hates them?
Someone they hate?

Do they even care?
Can you live in this country and
not
care,
not feel the tension of these
remarkable differences
or remarkably not so different
differences
weighing
        weighing?

I can feel the air leaking from me.
I'm all a-shake
        and a-jitter.
I hate this.
The sun burns the top of my head,
and I'm starting to see black spots
in front of my eyes.
Then I spy
a small silver car signaling to turn
onto this little stretch of road.
Still scared,
I step out of the post's shelter
to see.

There's a dark blue logo of some sort
painted on the hood of the car.
It turns, and I can hear the stutter of the motor
as it pulls up to me
and stops.
The same logo is painted on the passenger door,
and I can make out the Hebrew letters,

כ א

kaf aleph
Kfar Avivim.
I grab my bags
and walk to the door
slowly
        hesitantly
and look in the window.
There's an older man with
white hair and a beard.
Not really what I expected,
but he looks harmless enough.
He beckons to me to come closer.
The window rolls down automatically.
You're going to the kibbutz?
he asks, with
a clipped English accent

like birdsong.
I nod my head, swallowing.
Well, come on, then.
I open the trunk,
heave my suitcase and duffel bag in
and climb into the car.
Here we go
again.

KFAR AVIVIM

His beard is neatly trimmed
and his hair thinning on top.
You're new, eh? he asks,
sounding mildly disinterested.
Y-yes, I reply,
with a slight tremor in my voice.
A volunteer, I suppose?
I nod, mmm-hmming.
Well, I'm Henry, he says.
And your name would be?
Sarah. I pause. *You live on the kibbutz?*
Oh, yes. I moved here . . .
he pauses, murmuring to himself,
mmm, going on forty years ago now.
I have come here expecting to meet
a tanned Israeli man,
a strong one, who works the land.
And instead, I meet *Henry*?
An immigrant?

With a fancy accent?
Not exactly what I imagined I'd find here.

Henry drives very slowly,
often jerking the gear shifts unevenly,
as though he's scared of the car.
Or the road.
Well, here's the security gate.
I'll drive you to the dining hall.
You'll meet Rachel, the volunteer coordinator there.
She'll take care of you, he tells me.
The gate is painted bright yellow
with bars like a prison door.
Who are they trying to keep out?
Even here, in the middle of the countryside,
they
      we
must wall ourselves in?
The taste of sorrow creeps to my tongue,
but I swallow it as
we drive by fields and rundown buildings,
ramshackle steel and concrete constructions.
What's this?
      Ah-ha, I've found
      my voice!

I ask, pointing out the window.
That's our factory. For irrigation pipes.
Mostly outsiders from town
work there now, he replies.
We pull up in front of a huge white building
standing on stilts
like fat elephant legs.
Here we are. I'll just park,
then I'll show you
where to go.
Clumsily, he swings the car into a spot
and strains as he helps me pull
my belongings from the trunk.
Then we walk to the underbelly of the dining hall.
The ground is paved with a
macadam of tiny pebbles and gravel.
The suitcase wobbles jerkily, and Henry
shoots me a withering look.
I can feel my ears start to burn.
Another person who thinks I'm a jerk
for bringing too much stuff.
This is Rachel's office, he says,
as he knocks on a closed wooden door.
Yes! a sharp,
parrotlike voice calls.

We enter the cramped office,
and Henry tells the woman sitting at the desk
that he's brought her fresh meat.

     Great.

It was nice to meet you.
Best of luck, Sarah.
And Henry turns to leave.

Rachel is brusque, and she leads me quickly
around the kibbutz.

I hardly focus on my surroundings,
just Rachel's broad back.

She shows me the closet where I can
find work clothes.

I'm allowed to choose whatever I want
from an array of stained and
torn khakis, jeans, and T-shirts.

They share clothes here?

Ew.

The job schedule:
I'm to start working in the fields.

We work six days a week
from dawn till noon,
and I'm allowed
an extra day off

every month.
And my room.
It's dingy and gray
with a stone floor and a screen door
with a curtain on the inside.
And a small window.
Rachel tells me, as she departs,
The other volunteer rooms
are behind yours.
Most of them are still
at work, though
some may be at the swimming pool.
It's just up the road, and around to the left
I should ask for directions if I can't find it.

Kibbutz,
a communal society,
a farm,
from which everyone takes,
on which everyone lives
　　　from each according to his ability
　　　and to each according to his need.
It's foreign
and beautiful

and depressing
all at once.
The graying mattress on the cot
is about four fingers high.
I start to think lovingly of my bedroom
at home,
painted a cheery blue,
the color of the sky,
with a thick rug and
bright white curtains.
And my bed, thick and comfortable,
littered with pillows.
My own, private nest.
Where I don't have to share dirty
clothes
or mattresses
with strangers.
Where I have my own car to drive
   I'm not even allowed
   to take out one of the cars
   that belong to the kibbutz.
Trapped here,
like a fish in a tank.
   Alone.

But I'll be working in the fields
    the land
    of the Jews.
Land that should be mine.
Land that doesn't make me feel
alien.
Rather,
like I belong.
I'm going to dig my fingers into this soil.

THE FISH TANK
AND OPEN SPACE

There is a small, upright wardrobe closet
facing the bed.
Plastic-plated wood
peeling from the corners,
and the shelf at the bottom lined with
a soft gray layer of dust and dirt
and the shriveled-up
dried-out skeletons of dead insects
that mistakenly wandered in
once.
I begin to empty my clothes into it,
but I only have three plastic hangers.
Most of my things will stay in the suitcase
I guess.
What did I get myself into?
I brought a photo of my parents
and one of Annie and Alice,
and I place them on
the little wooden shelf

above my bed.
I don't have frames
so they slide down
against the wall
and fall.
I pick up the pictures
and replace them.
The sheets I took from the volunteers' closet
are rough and spotted.
I spread them over the bed
and line my shoes up against the wall.
Home for the next two and a half months.

I pull on a bathing suit and step out.
The sun is still burning hot,
and I am momentarily blinded, like a mole
emerging from its dark underground chamber.
The path is gray, gravelly, and I can feel the heat
seeping through the soles of my sandals.
Giant plants that I've never seen before
with long green leaves like tentacles
and tall bushes with dainty white blossoms
line the edges of the path
and shield whatever lies on the other side
from my sight.

I pass a dome-shaped structure
     like an igloo built of
     smooth, slate-colored stones
that is covered
with fiery pink bougainvillea.
A rusted metal door with a small
darkened window
stands on guard.
I stop to look at it,
wondering what it could possibly be.
Then it occurs to me,
as I peer through the dirty glass
at the stairs leading down and down
into the earth.
     It's a bomb shelter.
I look around to see if anyone is coming.
No one in sight.
I place my palm,
fingers splayed over the grooves and
cracks in the stone,
against the side of the shelter.
I put my other hand on the other side
and I hoist myself up,
scaling the rounded wall
till I am sitting on top

like the caterpillar on his toadstool,
and the view is spectacular.
Taupe-colored stucco houses
nest close to one another,
as though huddling together
through a battering storm,
with television antennae scrambling from the roofs
like waving arms,
like crazy arms.
And untidy yards below,
littered with plastic playgrounds
and soccer balls,
messy gardens of rosebushes
and wildflowers.

REMEMBERING, PART 4

Open space.
Acres and acres of vast green fields.
Three acres was a lot, but it seems
so much smaller now.
I used to run through the land surrounding our house,
exploring rabbit holes and my mom's
tomato patch and
the cornfield filling our backyard.
> Planting corn was quite a coup
> for a pair of Jews from the city.
With the smell of manure gently lingering in the air,
my father would drive a large red tractor
through our meadow,
cutting down grass and wildflowers
in neat rows.
I used to love sitting up there
in front of him,
> high up there on the tractor,

watching the blades slice through the tall grasses.
We were the masters of the fields then.

I loved the freedom of the open space.
I loved the meadow
and I loved the soil.

We're the only Jews for miles,
my parents, displaced New Yorkers
uprooted and replanted in the countryside,
and I'm one of two in my class.
Our house tucked snugly into the valley,
and the neighbors always coming by,
inviting us to church.
Then there was Michele from my
fifth-grade class
who once told me so nonchalantly
that I'd be going to hell when I died,
since I didn't accept Jesus into my heart.
Difference isn't accepted,
it certainly isn't appreciated
where I'm from.
There's just, more
or less,

fear.

And it swallows up the openness of the fields

and it drains the beauty from the land.

And I knew, I always knew that

no matter how much I loved the woods

and the hills surrounding our valley,

and the meadows and the dirt,

this land would never be mine.

Nor the people.

    And that's lonely.

SWIMMING WITH STRANGERS

I slide back down,
off the bomb shelter,
knocking loose a shower of
small pebbles,
and wipe my hands on the back of my shorts.
The path is a dead end.
Did Rachel say to go left or right?
I can't remember, but I veer to the left.
Suddenly, the sound of children
squealing and shouting with laughter
bursts through
a thicket of trees.
I follow it.
Then I see the pool
     dozens of children and parents
     splashing and lounging in the sun
     and under the farthest umbrellas,
     a group of teenagers and people who look
     maybe just older than I.

I start to feel nervous again,
always shy around new people.
What if they're all Israeli and don't
speak English?
Or won't?
What if they see a dork,
what if I'm marked?
With a scarlet *D*
and a marching band uniform
branded onto my skin.
And they'll see this scared, shy girl
coming at them,
who doesn't speak their language,
who wouldn't know what to say anyway.
But I steel myself.
There's more here than just a girl
who's too afraid to talk.

If I'm not a dork,
I'm certainly a coward.
After one look around,
I hightail it back to my room
and long for
the pool back home,

blue and glistening with
black painted lines, where
it's likely that Alice and Annie
are sitting along the edge,
watching over screaming children
playing in the water.
  My two best friends
   for as long as I can remember.

REMEMBERING, PART 5

The three of us sat in a row
in the football stadium bleachers,
Annie, Alice, and I, all
in our marching band uniforms,
feather-plumed hats, and
clarinets in our laps.
And somehow, I didn't
feel so self-conscious
in that heavy, manly uniform
when they were beside me.
Alice would reach over
and squeeze my hand comfortingly
whenever Stephanie and Jake's
eyes met across the fence
separating the cheerleaders from
the football field.
They knew of my crush.
They never mocked,
though all three of us

knew
     wouldn't admit
it was hopeless
        -ly
   absurd.
Then we would retreat to
Annie's house in the afternoons
following the games,
and play trios,
Beethoven and Brahms,
finding ourselves
as we wanted
and wished we could be
in the
delicacy,
the grace
of the music
and our notes flowing
through and in between one another,
coming together
in the textures of three.

  Now they are probably playing duets.

THE DINING HALL,
OR *HEDER OCHEL*

I wait until six o'clock,
dinnertime.
When my stomach is too empty
and complaining
to skip another meal,
to miss making an entrance at the dining hall.
I make my way along the
bare paths
to the looming white building.
The dining area,
I'm alarmed to see, very closely
resembles my high school cafeteria.
I stand on a line to take a plastic tray
and silverware,
fork tines bent and crooked.
Now my stomach is
really growling and grouching.
It's been neglected all day.
But then I look around at the trolleys of food.

There's nothing to eat.
No, that's an exaggeration.
There are raw vegetables.
Carrots and cucumbers and tomatoes.
There are bins filled with creamy, yogurtlike substances
in white and pink.
And there are baskets of sliced bread.
A field of long tables
and plastic chairs
lined up in neat rows.
I spot Henry
sitting with three other adults
all dressed in shorts and worn-out sandals.
I sit at a table by myself,
not too far from
the same group of teens I saw at the pool.
I can overhear snatches of conversation,
Hebrew and English mixed.
There are four boys, all with
bodies that boys
in my high school
haven't developed,
well-defined muscles
that show through their tight T-shirts
and tans.

They look to be
a few years older than I,
probably just out of the army.
They are speaking in Hebrew
to each other,
laughing, eyes dancing.
There are four girls, too.
They are all speaking English.
Two of them, blondes,
have some sort of accent,
the third girl sounds British,
and the fourth sounds American.
One of the blonde girls with the funny accent
glances over at me and smiles.
A cold smile
that does not reach
her eyes.
She waves and calls to me,
Hey, are you the new volunteer?
I nod my head, stand, and move closer.
What's your name? she asks.
Her accent is vaguely English, but harsher somehow.
Sarah. What's yours?
Jessie.

Are you a volunteer? I venture.
Yeah, all of us girls are. The boys are from here.
You're American, huh?
Another cruel half-smile whispers across her lips.
Yeah. What about you? I ask,
Where are you from?
Me and Julie are from South Africa.
She waves her hand
towards the other blonde.
The other two, Karen and Katie,
are English and Canadian.
I look at the other girls.
Julie and Karen are now absorbed
in conversation with the boys,
clearly flirting,
willowy fingers winding locks of hair,
twisting around,
touching tanned arms.
Featherlike caresses.
Giggles and lowered lashes.
Jessie turns away from me
to resume talking to one of the Israeli boys,
whose hair is
closely cropped to his head,

with sunglasses are perched
on the crown of his head
　　　like Lior wears his.
Katie, the fourth girl, a heavy girl,
looks bored.
I lower myself into a faded blue plastic chair
between Katie and Julie.
I have a cucumber, a tomato, a carrot,
and two slices of bread on my plate,
and some of the pink goo in a bowl.
　　　I guessed correctly.
　　　It's strawberry yogurt.
I watch the others to see what they
are doing with their vegetables.
Because I can't imagine sitting here
and biting into my carrot,
saying, *What's up, Doc?*
Everyone is busy sawing away
at the cucumbers and tomatoes
with blunt butter knives.
Dicing them up into even cubes.
It's amazing how uniform everyone's
vegetables are.
One of the boys is pouring olive oil
over his salad with the earnest diligence

of a worker ant.
They have all avoided the carrots,
and now I'm not sure what to do with mine.
I push it from my plate onto the plastic tray
so no one can see that I didn't know
what I was doing,
so they can't see that I took a carrot.
I begin to cut my cucumber and tomato
into cubes
like the others.
It's not as easy as it looks.
The knife slips, and somehow
I manage to cut my thumb,
even though the blade is barely sharp.

     I can't believe that this is all they eat here.
The girls are talking to the boys.
And I've been forgotten.
I turn to Katie.
She has nice eyes that don't match the
sour expression
twisted across her mouth.
She has cherry-red lips, though.
Hi, I try.
Hi. Her face softens. *So, whereabout
in America are you from?*

She's from Canada.

I can tell immediately.

She has that funny way of saying about

    a-boot.

I'm from Pennsylvania, a couple of

hours from Philadelphia. What about you?

I'm from Toronto,

she tells me.

How long have you been here? I ask.

Hmmm. It's been about six months, I guess.

You just got here? she says.

Yeah.

I pause, thinking

she's been here for six months?

Doesn't she have family,

friends in Canada?

I thought the other volunteers would be students,

like me, here for the summer

and ready to return

in the fall.

But they all look older.

Then I wonder,

maybe I could be lucky

and meet someone else who has to wake up

at the crack of dawn tomorrow,

who will show me what to do in the fields,
who will be a friend.
Where do you work? I ask.
It varies. Usually I'm in the fields,
but sometimes I work in the laundry,
which is the worst, she says.
The worst? I ask.
Personally, I hate doing laundry more than anything,
but some people
      like my mom
seem to enjoy it.
        She says it's relaxing.
The place is filled with old ladies,
who listen to classical music or
talk radio,
and we fold clothes
and towels
and sheets
all day long,
and they're stingy with the breaks
and never let me out for lunch
when everyone else eats.
She lowers her voice,
Not that hanging around this bunch
is very exciting, anyway.

So, I guess it really doesn't
matter much.
My voice drops to a whisper. *Why?*
What's going on?
And why does she stay
if she thinks it's so bad?
Look around. All the girls do here is flirt.
And the boys are gross.
They just
want to sleep with the girls.
They think they're easy.
And they're right.
All a guy has to say
is he's in the army, or he's
going to the army,
and the girls fall all over him.
My ears burn, and some kind of a lump
lodges itself in my throat.
Is that what Lior thinks of me?
Am I such a sucker?
And they have sex?
I know I shouldn't
be surprised, because
I know a lot of the kids
in my school

do it,
but it feels
      I feel
like it's wrong
      for me
now.
It's what older people
      who aren't my parents
do.
And suddenly, this budding friendship
with a Canadian girl whose
name I've only just learned
is cut short,
like a grape severed from its vine,
before it's had the chance to ripen.
She'll think I'm just one of these silly girls.
And I've always thought I was so much smarter
than the girls at school, the cheerleaders,
like Stephanie,
who only seem to care about boys
and hair.
Now it's clear.
I'm just as foolish.
I guess boys do that to girls.
All it took for me

was one cute, tanned Israeli boy,
with a rifle slung over his shoulder,
fatigues and dog tags,
and warm, chocolate eyes.
Not a jock, not a nerd.
Almost a man.
One Jewish boy,
who's so different from the boys at home.
But maybe not so different.

     I remember Jake.
So, what's your name, anyway?
The Canadian breaks into my thoughts.
Oh, it's Sarah. You're Katie?
She nods and smiles, and it's a kind smile.
I'm surprised, after her grousing.
I wonder how old she is
and if she's sad.
And I'm sad for her, just in case.
The other girls are ignoring me
and her
in favor of the boys.
But I catch a few of those boys
studying me,
watching me,
unabashedly, most of them,

one out of the corner of his eye.
But I like to feel their eyes on me
anyway.
No longer invisible.
Powerful,
a little bit.
As we finish up our dinners,
Katie leans over to whisper in my ear,
Next is the bonfire. You should see this.
I'll even come, too.
For your induction.
My induction?
What? I mumble, my mouth filled
with crunchy, sloppily diced cucumbers,
tomato juice threatening to fly
from between my lips.
You'll see.
You'll see just
how provincial these people are.
I can't help but wonder again
why she's stayed here
for six months if
she hates it so much.
We stand up all together,
the bunch of us,

and carry our plastic trays and dishes
into the kitchen, where a
long metal conveyer belt
runs lazily along
a polished chrome track
that winds into the
unseen bowels of
the kitchen.
Red milk crates swing by
and we stack our dishes
and trays in them.

THE BONFIRE

The twilit sky has begun to darken.
The warm air is still.
I follow the group, Katie walking beside me,
as we cross out of the dining hall area
and into the middle
of one of the clusters
of beige, muddy houses.
Some of the houses are
connected and they face
another row, and
there is a grassy lawn
in between them.
We walk through this cluster
into the next.
There I see the remnants of a fire,
a circle of rocks surrounding a
pile of burnt sticks
in a bare, charred patch in the grass.
Everyone takes a seat around the campfire spot.

There are more milk crates to sit on, and a log,
and one boy emerges from a house with two
six-packs of beer in his hand.
He passes the bottles around,
and everyone takes one,
but me.
I've never had a beer.
I can't have beer
          legally
          at home.
But this isn't home—though
I don't know if it's illegal here, too,
but no one else seems concerned.
I feel everyone looking at me,
expectantly,
so I pull a bottle from the carton and
continue passing it.
My heart is beating so hard,
I think it must be audible.
What do I do?
I can't have beer,
my parents would kill me.
I juggle the cold bottle
from hand to hand.
The boys set to work lighting the fire.

They're still somewhat indistinguishable to me,
wearing raggedy T-shirts
with the necks cut off, so that they hang wide,
almost about their shoulders,
tight across their chests,
and ratty jeans and sandals.
Their toes are uniformly brown
and callused
with white cracks of wear,
heads crew cut
     because they're a crew
     a gang
     of boys
     from the army?
with sunglasses perched like crowns of laurel.
They are dark with dark eyes,
but one has eyes of piercing blue
that shine in the growing dusk.
They gather sticks
as three girls huddle together on the log,
and Katie and I on milk crates
next to each other.
Another boy leaves one of the houses
with a can of gasoline.
Soon the fire is leaping into the air

with orange claws curling, tearing at the darkness.
Everyone is drinking, and the blonde girls,
Julie and Jessie, are
          the only word I can think of
gabbing,
their English bent and brief,
harsh.
I don't like the sound of it.
Come on, teach us some Hebrew we can really use,
Jessie giggles.
Efo ha heder ohel?
          Where is the dining hall?
she says, in the strongest
South African accent she can muster.
The boys laugh,
clearly charmed.
Come on, we want to know how to talk like
real Israelis.
Teach us,
Jessie coos.
For example, look at Yossi here,
one of them answers, pointing to his friend.
He's a tembel, a stupid,
and the Hebrew teacher cracks up
at his own wittiness.

Tembel, Jessie mimics.

Tembel, Julie echoes.

Both girls giggle some more.

Katie catches my eye and rolls her own.

She turns away from the fire

and slurps on her beer.

Those girls are goofy,

transparent,

but what's with Katie?

If Lior was here,

he would put his arm around me.

And we'd sit and talk,

and I wouldn't feel

so foolish.

I look to the English girl sitting nearest

to me on the log.

She smiles at me,

almost ruefully, and shrugs.

I'm Karen, she says.

I'm Sarah, I answer.

I take a drink from my bottle.

It's so bitter.

I didn't realize, and I

almost spit it out.

Why do people drink this stuff?

The blue-eyed boy stands up,
holding a stick
the length of my forearm.
Now we play, he says seriously,
Stick Alive.
Katie mutters, *Here we go.*
I start to feel nervous,
as I watch him thrust the
stick into the fire.
He pulls it out and the tip is
glowing red.
Stick alive, he repeats,
then passes the stick to Yossi,
who takes it and passes it quickly to
the Hebrew teacher next to him,
who nearly throws it at Jessie,
and the stick makes its way around the circle.
I have no idea what is supposed to happen.
We just sit here,
silently passing the stick
around and around.
Finally, the end of the stick goes dark.
Yossi is holding it,
and his face falls.
The boy next to him snorts,

and the others jeer at him
in Hebrew,
snickering and laughing.
Yossi stands up
and says, *Stick dead.*
Then he brushes the burnt
end of the stick over each cheek,
leaving streaks of charcoal
across his face
like war paint,
and he drinks his beer,
finishing it in a long series of deep
gulps.
Oh, it's like Hot Potato.
>With a fiery stick
>and alcohol.
We play again and again,
and I don't want to have to paint my face.
Soon Karen has her stripes
and the Hebrew teacher
and Blue Eyes.
And then, next thing I know, I'm
holding the stick, and the orange
tip sizzles to black
as I'm trying to pass it to Katie.

She shakes her head at me,
tilting her eyebrows to signal
that I'm stuck with it.
I stand up, and I can hear my voice shake.
Stick dead.
And I draw the stick over my cheeks,
praying the ashes won't
make me break out tomorrow,
but I find that the war stripes
make me feel different.

      Powerful

      Primitive

      Primal

And I grab my bottle and take a deep swig.
The boys clap for me,
and Blue Eyes smiles appreciatively,
and the boy who's been
watching me
since dinner
rises to his feet and gives an ovation.
Then they start chattering to each other
in Hebrew again,
excitedly.
We're going to the Yarden,
Blue Eyes says authoritatively.

And everyone is on their feet, running.
We head back towards the dining hall,
and I turn to ask Katie what's going on.
But she's not with us.
I see her walking in the opposite direction
alone.
So I catch up with Karen and ask her.
We're going to the Yarden, she answers.
The what? I ask, feeling stupid.
The river. The Jordan River. It's fun, don't worry.
She looks at me reassuringly.
We get to the parking lot in front of the *heder ochel,*
and everyone piles into an old VW van,
the kind with the rounded roof.
It's yellow and white,
and it looks about a million years old.
I'm starting to feel a bit dizzy, nauseated,
and remembering that I just chugged a bottle of beer,
I sway as I try to climb into the van.
Come on, Sarah, the boy
who stood up and clapped for me says,
as he reaches down a hand to pull me in.
How does he know my name?
We cram into the seats, eight of us.
Blue Eyes is at the wheel,

and we peel out of the parking lot,
down the narrow kibbutz road,
to the yellow security gate.
It's closed, and Yossi hops out of the front seat
and fiddles with a control box outside,
and the gate creaks open.
The van tips and sways as we
leave the kibbutz behind.
We're driving on tiny, curved roads
that wrap around hills and hug clifftops
that dip into deep ravines.
I'm scared, but everyone around me is laughing,
and I feel like I should be enjoying this.
This adventure, this fun
that I never have at home.
There,
we don't paint our faces with
ash.
I've never felt so
accepted
so fast.
It's always been a fight
to prove to everyone and to me
that I am good enough,
fun enough.

And here we are in this ancient van,
racing through the dark
in this ancient land,
and they want me here.
I like the attention.
I like that Nadav (I heard
one of the others
call him
by his name) watches me.
Until I came to Israel,
boys didn't even notice me.
Why can't I feel brave?
Why can't I let go and enjoy this?
I close my eyes and let the wind
that streams through the open windows
blow against my face,
and I stop thinking.
I imagine I can hear music,
a slow guitar
crying softly
laughing gently
as I feel I am awakening
from a deep sleep
of sixteen years.

THE RIVER

Blue Eyes, whose name is
Roi, like *row-ee*,
gathers us at the edge
of the river.
It's so dark now,
I can only see the stars
gleaming clear in the cool black sky.
And the river
dancing and weaving in the starlight.
And a cold, silvery moon hangs
over it all.
The girls sit on a cement slab
next to the water,
as the boys forage for more wood
and build up another bonfire.
Roi pulls out a blackened pot
from a small backpack
and pours some water from a plastic bottle
into it, a bag of coffee grounds,

then puts the pot on top of
a small butane burner.
A blue flame escapes into the dark night,
and the earthy smell of coffee mixes with
the scent of honeysuckle.
I breathe deeply and think I
may never smell this mix of earth and sky again.
I never did before.
Nadav pulls several small glasses
from the backpack and places them
on the ground.
Then he turns to me and says,
We make coffee like the Bedouins.
It has to boil seven times.
Then it is ready.
It's a tradition.
Roi pours the coffee into the glasses
after it has cooked seven times over the small flame,
and he adds two lumps of sugar into each,
and stirs, then passes the glasses
around,
first to the girls, then to the boys.
Roi's face is earnest
as he tells me,
The coffee has to rest, so it can fall

to the bottom.
Then we sit around the bonfire, which is
now roaring,
and sip on our coffee
that is brewed in the ancient
way of the Bedouins,
the glasses too hot to hold
very long.
The liquid scalds the tip of my tongue
but tastes so good.
Sweet and thick,
it coats my tongue and throat
like syrup.
And a rich brown silt
collects in the depths
of the glass.
Suddenly, Roi stands up
and shouts,
Whose birthday is it?
Yossi crows in answer,
It's Adi's birthday!
Then Roi and Nadav
and Yossi rise and
grab Adi the Hebrew teacher
under his arms

and by the legs and race
down to the bank of the river,
whoop, *Happy birthday!*
and toss Adi into the water.
He gives a yell, then falls with a splash,
and sits up, wiping his eyes.
The water is shallow.
It barely covers his legs.
He stands, shaking his head, laughing.
Then he races to Nadav and throws
him into the river.
Happy birthday! Adi crows.
Nadav rises, dripping,
and comes to where I'm sitting.
It's your birthday, I think.
        A Cheshire cat.
Uh-uh, no way,
I say.
Suddenly, I'm in Nadav's arms and he
is tossing me through the air
and into the river,
which is freezing.
Happy birthday, Sarah!
all of the boys scream,
laughing hysterically.

My clothes are heavy with water,
but I lie on my back and push my head
below the surface and look at the stars,
blurred and streaky,
and pick up my head and breathe.
I'm so cold,
but it doesn't matter.
I am like the minnows darting past my fingers,
liquid silver
free.
I sit up and laugh
and it feels so good to laugh like this,
wild, like a yell,
out of control,
to match my war stripes.
Adi gives me a hand out of the water.
The slope up to the concrete is slippery,
and we slide down together and fall
back into the water.
We're all giggling, but
I'm shivering,
and Roi grabs a musty blanket from the van,
which he gives me.
I wrap myself up,
hover in front of the fire,

sipping my now lukewarm coffee,
granules of grinds coating my teeth,
a taste of a summer yard and
faraway forbidden places.
The other girls seem to have taken a
new interest in me.
Now that my acceptance
has been confirmed
by the boys,
I suppose.
Where in America are
you from?
Karen asks.
Without waiting for
my answer, Jessie
pounces,
How old are you?
Her eyes narrow,
and she licks her lips
      like a cat
                anticipating my answer.
Sixteen. How old are you? I ask
as sweetly as I can.
Oh, you're a baby, she
smirks. *Julie and I are nineteen.*

You can't even drink a beer in America,
can you? Julie asks, wide-eyed.
I nod my head,
feeling somewhat rebellious, and
proud of it.
Americans are so puritanical,
Jessie pipes up.
Yeah, Julie echoes.
　　　　(Good answer, Julie.)
They're immature, too,
Jessie hisses.
Oh shut up. You're the immature one,
Karen hushes her. Jessie
sits back,
licking her wounds,
eyes narrowed to slits
darting my way.
Why are girls so mean to each other?
Why do they take every opportunity to
make other girls feel bad?
Do I do that?
I just can't imagine it.
I couldn't bring myself to bare
my claws and teeth,
swipe

at someone like that.
Karen tells me to ignore them,
that they're just jealous.
Of what? Julie asks,
indignant.
Of her American blue jeans and her
pretty green eyes
and all the boys looking at her,
Karen sneers.
I don't know what to do.
I suspect Karen
aims only to
insult
the South African girls.
Suddenly I'm swimming
in loneliness,
stuck here
with these catty, nasty girls,
and all of the joy of the evening is
sucked away
in the vacuum of girls being girls.
They are mean,
but we are here
in this place
together.

We return to the van,
its dirty cream-colored vinyl
seat sticking to my wet jeans.
The boys are singing
some song in Hebrew,
and they're very silly.
The girls are silent.
I, too.
Now we turn left where
we turned right on our way
to the Yarden River,
and climb where the road dropped
before.
We return to the kibbutz
and leave the van in the parking lot.
The other girls bid their good-nights
to the boys,
wordlessly pairing off,
melting into the darkness.
I spy Jessie kissing Adi,
and he grasps her,
hands groping
about her waist.
Karen and Roi
stand next to the van,

as he jingles the keys in
one hand and cups her face
with his other.
She murmurs softly into his ear,
while Julie and Yossi kiss sloppily
and shamelessly
in the middle of the parking lot.
Nadav eyes me.
I can feel my cheeks heat up
and my palms start to sweat.
I kissed Lior good-bye just
this morning.
It already seems like
an eternity ago.
I have never kissed
two boys
in one day.
Ever.
I nod to him,
thinking, hoping
he'll turn
and go, but
he comes near.
I know he can sense my
nervousness.

He extends his hand
as if to shake mine,
and clumsily
draws me into an embrace.
Lilah tov, *Sarah,*
he whispers.
Good night, Nadav.
My voice is shaky
  relieved
    prickly
  regretful
uncomfortable.
Am I being disloyal to Lior?
Not if he's like
those soldiers on the bus.
I don't want to believe he's like that.
Still.
I do like feeling Nadav's arms around me.
Like an electric cord
stretching from Nadav to me,
something in my stomach twitches
and draws me further into his arms.
Something that makes me want to
stay there,
close to him,

for a long time.
He gently plants a kiss on my forehead.
Then we quietly make our way back
to our separate rooms.
I check my watch.
It's nearly one o'clock.
I have to be at work in
four hours.
I wash my face and teeth
and go to bed.
And suddenly, I feel
so tired.

HI-HO, HI-HO,
IT'S OFF TO WORK . . .

It's 4:30 when my alarm screeches,
yanking me from sleep
like an icy claw.
I walk to the window,
draw back the curtain.
It's still dark outside,
and I can see the stars,
clear and cold
like the dawn air,
blanketing the sky.
Hastily, I throw on my
adopted work clothes,
raggedy blue jeans
with a hole over the left knee
and a camel
someone drew below the right front
pocket
in black magic marker,
a stretched-out, white T-shirt,

and big brown work boots.
I clomp my way over to the dining hall,
where I see Jessie, Karen, and Julie
      Katie must be in the laundry today
huddled at a table
sleepily, silently nursing cups of coffee.
And there is a middle-aged man
with a mane of scruffy white hair
that barely licks his shoulders,
sharp but gentle deep-set eyes,
and a hooked nose that
gives him the profile of an eagle.
Sarah?
he asks.
His voice is surprisingly soft.
Yes.
Shmuel?
He nods.
Shmuel is the overseer of the fields.
Take some coffee. We don't come back
till ten o'clock
for breakfast, he
instructs me.
I take a plastic mug from a teetering pile,
two spoons of

instant coffee, Nescafé,
as they call it here
    it means miracle coffee
two lumps of sugar,
and a drop of milk,
mix it all together,
    spoon clanging like a church bell,
as I saw the boys do at dinner last night.
Then add hot water.
I sit down at the end of the table
next to Julie.
The coffee has a funny aftertaste
that reminds me of the glue
my father and I used
to construct model dinosaurs
    when I was younger.
No one speaks.
I wonder if the other girls feel as bad
as I do,
queasy and empty,
having gotten only three hours of sleep.
I wonder if you get used to it here,
not sleeping.
At home my parents always
make me

get into bed by eleven
on weekdays,
insisting I need to be
fully
rested
for school.
They never said anything about
feeling well enough for
manual labor, though.
Shmuel watches us closely
but not uncomfortably,
and when we've finished our coffee,
he tells us it's time to go.
Outside in the parking lot,
Shmuel gets on top of a tractor
and we climb into a trailer hitched to the back.
The tractor bumps down a dirt trail
lined with stones and tall grass,
and we come to the crest of a hill.
I can see the valley spreading out below,
all yellow with dried-out summer grasses
and patches of green
where the fields are,
and I can see the thin blue-brown ribbon of
the Yarden River

and one violet mountain standing to the north
all by itself.
Once we reach the bottom of the ravine,
Shmuel hands out knives and work gloves.
And he walks over to a bright green plant
with thick leaves
heavy with juices,
growing close to the ground.
He cuts off a limb of the plant,
and now I can see that it is aloe.
Shmuel splits the piece lengthwise
and offers a half to me.
Here, take this. Rub it on your skin.
It will keep away the mosquitoes.
He cuts more for the other girls, and I
watch as they rub the aloe
all over their arms and necks,
and I do the same,
cringing at the feel of its cool stickiness.
Shmuel walks over to the edge of the field.
It is a cornfield,
and we are to pull up the weeds growing between
the stalks.
His eyes are closed, and he appears to be
concentrating very closely.

His eyes open and catch mine watching him.
Can you hear the wolf crying? he asks.
A small smile crosses his mouth.
I stop moving and listen.
There it is, a mournful howling
that sends a chill up my spine.
I wonder what he's crying for.
I never heard a wolf in real life before.
How close is he?

>Do wolves feed on new American
>girls, who can't
>understand the ways of this country?

I bend back to the weeds.
They are small, and sometimes
hard to distinguish from the foliage
of the corn stalks.
I squat, carefully using my knife to
wheedle the weeds
from their tough grasp on the soil.
My knees grow sore, and I stand up,
but the other girls are working, working,
as though it's nothing.
I bend from the waist, but I can't
reach the ground easily,
and soon my back begins to hurt

worse than my knees.
I return to the squatting position and
make my way down the row,
looking up to see the other girls already
nearly done with their rows.
I hope I'll improve.
The sun has started on its course,
rising from the horizon, and the sky
is a hazy palette of rose and indigo.
A cloud of mosquitoes also comes up with the sun.
They buzz around my head,
and now I'm starting to feel warm.
A trickle of sweat
  worms
its
  way
down
my cheek,
and I want to wipe it away, but
my hands are melted to
the insides of the gloves.
I don't have
the energy to pull them off,
and I don't want to rub the dirt
clinging to my gloves onto my face.

I wish somebody would say something.
This is boring.
I always thought working the land
would feel good,
powerful, clean,
would make me feel strong.
Like I'd be claiming my own
piece of history.
But it's just hard.
Shmuel calls out,
Do you see the birds? Hawks
tracking their prey.
I look up, and against the now bright blue sky,
several birds,
nothing more than
charcoal smudges
silhouetted against the sky,
circle overhead.
I wonder who they're hunting.
Aren't they beautiful?
Shmuel asks no one in particular.
I look up at him and nod.
The mysterious smile,
a look of peace,
passes across his face again.

The sun starts to burn through the
early morning mists,
and I'm growing dizzy from
hunger and heat and,
hours
      though I'm not sure how many
of hard work,
bending over the soil,
tunneling through the narrow rows,
leaves and stems cutting my arms,
pulling at the stubborn green sprouts
that cling to the earth
for all that they are worth.
These scrawny little weeds,
crawling between the leaves
that are meant to be there.
Suddenly Shmuel breaks the
monotonous quiet, as he announces,
Let's go to breakfast.
Wearily we climb back into the tractor.
This time the bumps jar my joints,
yet it feels so good to be sitting.
I can't even summon the strength
to see the scenery.
We troop into the dining hall, and once again

I am amazed.

Breakfast is the same as dinner.

Raw vegetables,

cucumbers, tomatoes, and carrots,

pink yogurt, and bread.

      This time I avoid the carrots.

The boys come in and sit down with us.

I'm not sure where they've been working.

We can only muster nods of the head

in greeting.

Everyone bends

over their trays,

dicing vegetables, and I know Nadav

is looking at me again.

I can't bring myself to meet his gaze.

Just too tired.

It's too much.

This is all too much.

It's hard.

      I think I want to go home.

The air-conditioning in this stupid place

doesn't even work.

Sweat is beading across my forehead.

The Israelis,

I see in a sneaky glance around the table,

don't seem to sweat.
They look perfectly cool.
Maybe you have to be born here
to live like this.
And how am I supposed to work,
subsisting only on raw vegetables
and strawberry yogurt?

Karen, Jessie, and Julie
seem to have retrieved their will to live.
They are chattering with the boys.
Well, at least Jessie and Julie are.
Karen still looks a little weary.
I can't listen to them, though.
I start to imagine what the girls at home
are doing.
Annie and Alice are probably
at the pool with the kids they babysit.
No, probably still sleeping.
I should have just looked for
a job back there, too.
At least I'd be getting paid and
not slaving away
like this.
I wonder if they miss me?

I wonder if they even notice I'm
not around.
Our chemistry teacher took to calling
us the Summer Triangle,
after the constellation.
We were a formidable
lab team.
Trio.

As we finish our breakfasts,
Shmuel rises from a nearby table
and signals that it's time to go.
I surprise myself when an
audible groan
escapes from my lips.
I can have these sissy thoughts
in my head, but
I don't want anyone else to think
I'm just some spoiled American
who can't work.
I smile, so the others think I'm
only kidding.
I find Nadav's eyes on me
        still,
and in the morning light

I can see that they are hazel,
glowing yellow like a cat's.
And he gives me a warm,
comforting grin.
Yallah,
he says. Let's go.
And he stands up,
as though his going to work, too,
is in solidarity with me,
and it will make me feel better.
It kind of does.
We get back in the tractor,
and on the way down to the fields,
I'm once again able
to marvel at the beauty
of the countryside.
I try to comfort myself
with the thought that I'm working the
Jewish land.
As I return to the digging,
tearing at the tough little weeds,
and as I feel my fingers blistering
against the handle of my knife,
I start to feel that I can grow leaner
here.

I can do this.
I can work hard
with my hands.
And I can shed all the worries
and doubts
        at least for the time being
stop drowning in
all the stupid details
of life.
College
grades
friends
cheerleaders
and football players.
It's already beginning to be easy
to forget
all that junk
still exists for me.
Here, I listen to the birdsong
and watch a family of rabbits
poke their heads out of a
pile of wood stacked at the edge
of the field, which
Shmuel lovingly points out.
And I'll work this green patch

in the lake of yellow and brown
sun-dried land.
And my other life will
fall away
to an unreachable,
forgettable
distance.

I wonder where Lior is now,
what he's doing.
If he's okay.
If he's thinking of me.
Would he be impressed by
what I'm doing?
Probably not.
The army is probably a lot harder.
But I'm doing something
important, too.
Something good.
Maybe he'll call me.
Maybe I'll call him.

Jessie and Julie start to sing
a pop song
that I heard

on the radio at home.
Karen joins in,
her voice rough,
a bit off-key.
And I think, why not?
I sing along with them,
and soon, we've all forgotten the words
and repeat the chorus
over and over
then burst into a fit of giggles.
We poke our heads up
above the plants
to look at each other,
like prairie dogs emerging from their holes,
blinkingly into the light.
The latter part of the morning passes quickly,
and as the sun crosses to its zenith,
Shmuel tells us it's lunchtime.
Work is done for the day.
We return to the *heder ochel*
and I'm surprised to see that there aren't
any raw vegetables.
There is a hot food line, with rice
and some kind of meat.
There are cooked, spicy carrots

and chicken and more bread.
We sit down, and
it seems as though we've rediscovered
our energy.
Maybe we should go into town tonight,
Karen says.
Good idea. Where should we go?
Jessie asks.
We could get pizza! Julie exclaims.
Pizza . . .
How funny,
a pizzeria in
this place.

A HARD DAY'S NIGHT

After lunch,
I run back to my room
as fast as my weakened, achy
legs will carry me,
and I throw on my bathing suit,
which proves difficult
because I'm covered with grimy sweat,
aloe, and dirt.
It twists itself impossibly
                    around
                            my
legs
        and
I am seething with frustrationfury
by the time
I find myself scratching through
the hedges in front of the pool entrance.
There, Karen, Jessie, and Julie are

sunning their long, tanned
　　　perfect
bodies on worn towels next to the water.
I can't believe they aren't
in the pool.
I throw my towel and book down
on the ground beside them
and dive into the pool,
so sweaty and hot,
I don't care
what anybody thinks.
If I'm not acting proper.
This place isn't proper.
The water surrounds me with
a cool peace, and I wish
I could stay underwater forever.
My hair swims
around me, floatingframing my
face like a mermaid's.
When I climb out and drop
onto the ground, I
wrap the undersized
towel around myself.
The other girls' bodies look
so much more mature than mine.

My stomach and thighs feel
huge and my chest too tiny.
This self-consciousness,
like when I wear my band
uniform to school
and have to sit next to
a cheerleader in class.
Nadav and Adi enter the pool,
and I don't want them to
see me in my bathing suit, next to the
other girls in their bikinis.
I pick up my book and avoid looking at the boys.
But they come right over to us and
sit down.
Great.
It's unavoidable.
The boys will see me.
I keep my towel firmly wrapped
over my belly.
But then I start to sweat,
my body rebelling.
I reluctantly spread the towel
out on the grass and remain
buried in my book.
How was your first day of work?

Nadav's heavy accent breaks

my attempt at keeping the curtain down.

Um, it was good. It was hard,

but it was okay, I reply.

You were in the cornfields, right?

Yeah. Pulling up weeds, I answer.

Shmuel is a good man,

he tells me.

He seems nice.

All day he was pointing out

the birds and animals to us.

Nadav watches me.

I pick at the frayed edge of my towel.

I've noticed how much I

fidget around boys

since I arrived here.

Why do I do that?

I spot Katie entering the pool area.

I wave to her

and she nods to me,

then starts to walk over to us.

Nadav whispers to me,

She always looks so unhappy.

I think she doesn't

like it here, but
I don't know why she stays.
She never talks to anybody.
I tell him,
I wondered the same thing.
I feel bad for her,
but she doesn't seem to be interested.
She's funny and nice. I wish
she was happier.
You're a nice girl, Nadav says,
placing his hand over mine.
I pull away
and feel my face growing warm.
Nadav doesn't seem to notice.
He takes my hand again.
Why do you say that? You don't
even know me, I retort,
slipping my hand away again
I see you. I know you are.
That's all,
he says.
Then he springs to his feet,
his long, wiry body
moving with the grace of a panther

as he dives
into the deep end
of the pool.
Come on, Sarah, come in!
he calls.
I peer around,
though I'm not sure
what I'm looking for,
what kind of reassurance
I'll find.
The blondes are absorbed in
talking to Adi,
and Karen is reading a magazine,
though I suspect she is sleeping
behind her dark sunglasses.
I follow Nadav,
trying to imitate his dolphin dive,
but wind up feeling like a whale.
I look around for him
as I surface,
but he's nowhere.
Suddenly, a hand wraps around my ankle,
pulling me under.
I open my eyes in the water,

and Nadav is in front of me,
making faces.
I laugh, swim away,
and he darts after me,
but I'm a better swimmer.
I race him all around the pool.
He barely keeps up.
Finally, we climb out
into the dry
heat of the summer air
and find the others leaving,
returning to their rooms to
prepare for dinner.

     Except Katie, who is sitting
a little bit
apart,
reading a book.
I wonder what she's reading.
Why doesn't she make
even a little effort?
Nadav is drying himself off,
and he gathers his things.
See you soon, he tells me.
Are you coming into town? I ask.

Of course. How else
would you get there,
without us to drive you?
He smiles.
Then I'll see you soon.
I pick up my belongings, too,
but I stop by Katie before leaving.
Hi, how was your day? I ask.
It was okay. Boring as usual. Laundry,
she answers.
I figured,
when you weren't in the fields
with us, I say.
How was your day? she asks.
It was really hard, but it was
good. Um, are you going to
come into town with us
for dinner?
No, I'm going to go to bed early,
I think.
But thanks for asking.
Katie smiles at me warmly.
She isn't mean.
I just don't understand.

Why is she so bent
on being alone?
You sure? I ask.
She nods her head.
Okay, then. Have a good night, I say,
turning around to go.
I nearly skip
back to my room,
and while I shower,
I wonder what this night will bring.

PIZZA WITH A VIEW

Before I meet the others,
I run to the pay phone
in the dining hall.
I dial the number Lior gave me,
and after several stretched-out beeps,
he answers,
his voice gruff. *Hallo.*
Lior?
Yes, he answers.
It's Sarah.
Hi, he says.
How are you? Why
does my voice sound
like it's pleading?
Fine. Why is his voice
so sharp, his words short?
Um, that's good, I say. *I'm
on the kibbutz now. It's
beautiful here. The work is*

hard, but . . .
I'm babbling.
Like the blondes.
Then I hear, in the background,
what sound like catcalls
and chortling.
Lior cuts in. *Sarah,*
he says, *I have to go now.*
I'm sorry. I will call you later, okay?
I say, *Okay, I—*
Bye, he interrupts,
then the line clicks.
What happened?
Why did he sound so far away?
I imagine him in
his uniform.
He must be busy.
　　　But why were they laughing?
I replace the phone, then
pick it up again and dial
Michal's number.
Hallo, she answers after one beep.
Michal? Hi, it's Sarah.
Sarah, how are you? I'm so
glad you called. How is it there?

She truly sounds happy to hear
from me.
It's, it's hard. But I think
I like it here.
I worked in the fields, I tell her.
Yes, was it very hot? Did you
wear sunscreen?
Somehow these questions,
though there is a momentary
flicker of annoyance,
make me feel better.
Like my mom would have.
We talk some more,
then say good-bye,
promising to speak
every week.
I go outside,
where everyone is
congregated in the parking lot.
We get in the same van as last night
and leave the kibbutz.
Town is
a quaint village of stone villas
gracefully wrapped around a hill
that towers over the kibbutz

and surrounding fields.
The pizza restaurant is near the summit,
and the view is stunning.
A dusky light settles over the
land
and white and yellow lights twinkle in the
far-off hills of the Golan Heights,
giving them the appearance of
giant ships
harboring in a distant port.
The restaurant is nearly
empty, and it glitters with
candlelight and windows.
Jessie and Julie make endless
chatter with Yossi and Adi,
while Karen and Roi
nestle close to one another,
nuzzling, talking quietly.
It's beautiful, isn't it? Nadav
asks me.
He sits to my left,
and we are on a terrace
overlooking the sunset.
Yes, it is, I reply softly.
He takes my hand, holding it

between both of his.
Why isn't he
Lior?
Why can't I be sitting
at a table
with Lior
again?
Lior with his graceful hands,
long, lithe fingers.
    My first kiss.
But I don't pull away,
and I smile at him.
I try to picture Nadav in
a uniform like Lior's.
He finished the army
eight months ago.
I do like Nadav.
Oh, what's wrong with me?
I can hardly even remember
Lior's face now,
or being with him.
And Jake.
His face is merely
a blurry splotch.

High school feels eons away.
I'm glad of that.
I slip my hand from between Nadav's
and take a bite of my pizza.
It is delicious.
I am amazed,
sitting in a place so vastly
different from home,
and eating something so familiar.

THE ORCHARD

Instead of going back to the kibbutz,
we drive around it,
past the yellow gate
to another fence,
a chain-link fence,
held fast only by a padlock.
Roi pulls the van up to the
entrance and turns off the ignition.

He turns around in his seat
with a devilish grin
and says,
I want dessert.
Jessie, Julie, Karen, and I
give half-hearted shrugs.
Roi leaps from the van and
yanks open our door,
sliding it back with gusto.
Come! he cries.

We follow the boys and watch
as Adi picks the lock.
Finally, he swings open the gate,
and we file in behind him.
I don't know where we are.
Tall dark shapes loom overhead,
and suddenly Roi switches on
a flashlight.
It's an orchard.
Low-hanging boughs of
cool, smooth leaves
brush against my hair
and arms.
Nadav comes up next to me
and hands me something small
and leathery.
I try to see what it is in the dark,
but as I peer at it,
its shape only becomes
more indistinct.
It's a lychee,
Nadav tells me.
Eat it. It's a fruit.
I've never heard of a lychee before,

let alone eaten one.

Peel it and eat it.

I tear at the leathery skin,

and it comes away easily

in my fingers.

The fruit is slippery

but dry,

jellylike

but solid now.

Gingerly, I put it into my mouth.

The taste is as deliciously indescribably

ambiguous as the texture,

metallic and sweet and sour

and bland.

   Parasols and wooden walking sticks.

The exact taste eludes my tongue

and finds its way into my throat,

lodging there,

coating it.

Nadav's yellow cat eyes glint in

the dark,

holding the light of the flashlight

and reflecting it a million tiny times.

The taste, the feel of

the fruit is magical,
much like this orchard,
black with night,
heavy with the perfume of
enchanted air.
The eight of us begin tearing
the fruit off the trees,
gorging ourselves
on the berries,
stripping off the skins
and stuffing them into our hungry mouths.
We are silent,
and the only sounds are the shaking of the
branches,
the rustling of leaves,
the crunch of
our feet on the soft dirt.
Nadav is beside me.
I can feel him there,
like a current of electricity
whispering up and down the side of my arm.
He touches my hand, and
I turn to him.
Here, he says, and

places a lychee in my mouth,
his fingers delicately
lingering on my lips
as I take the fruit from him,
slowly letting my teeth break
the flesh open
in my mouth.
His fingers move to my cheek,
running over the skin,
the smell of the berries
clinging to his hand.
I close my eyes and will
myself to forget everything else.
This moment is too beautiful
to lose.

After we've had our fill, I
once again find myself standing
next to Nadav,
enveloped by the dark
of the parking lot,
as the other couples sigh their good-nights
and good-byes.
Are we a couple now?

He wraps his arms around me
and asks, as my muscles tense,
What are you frightened of, Sarah?
Do you have a boyfriend
back in America,
or something?
How do I answer this?
Is Lior a boyfriend?
I don't think so,
but some part of me feels unready
for this.
I—no, I don't have a boyfriend in America . . .
but, I . . .
This is fast
and powerful
and strange to me.
I look at him
sadly.
Is this the end,
the end of the fun we've had,
of this wonder?
Will he still want to talk to me?
It's okay, Sarah. I like you,
but

we're just having fun.
He leans down and kisses my cheek,
then turns and goes.
Tears fill my eyes and sting,
and I run back to my room.
I climb into bed and pull the thin
blanket over my head.
It will be terrible from now on.

AND DEATH,
HIS SILENT PARTNER

Things are not terrible.
Work is already routine
by this third day.
Exhausting,
stifling,
but I enjoy the
thoughtless
hours
under dawn's sun.
Emptied
of all but my senses.

Sweat burning my eyes
ears pricking at the baying wolves
turning the soil through gloved fingers
the decaying, living smell of the earth.
I am free.
Nadav smiles his easy
smile at lunch,
and spooning up

rice and lamb,
looking up at me,
he asks if I want to have dinner
outside the kibbutz.
Just us? I ask.
Just us, he replies.

After lunch I return
to my room,
the rough, nappy sheets
beckoning.
Part of me begs to
go to the pool,
to see what the others are doing,
but my body calls for sleep.
I drop onto the sheets,
muddy jeans, boots,
and all.

Nadav waits for me
outside my door,
leaning against
the porch rail.
He reaches out
to brush the scrubby bushes

lining the path.
He fingers
the petals of a small starlike flower
so gently.
He leads me to
a car parked in the lot,
and we drive in silence.
He passes the town and
drives up the great mountain.
The road twists and bends,
the car swerving close
to the edge of the precipice.
We drive and drive
for almost half an hour.
Still in silence.
Then we come to a large intersection.
Nadav's mouth turns down,
a frown darkening
the light that
usually dances in his eyes.
What's wrong? I ask.
There was a suicide bombing here,
about a year ago.
A bus.
He pauses.

My best friend was there.
He was killed.
Oh, Nadav, I start.
No, it's—I'm
okay, now.
It's—it was really bad.
But it's—
I'm
better now.
I don't know what to say.
What can I say?
I'm so sorry. It's—that's terrible.
I can't imagine . . .
I trail off.
I take his hand.
Nadav chews his bottom lip
slowly,
as though a thought
or memory
grasps at his mind
and won't let go.

And my mind is spinning.
What is this life?
What,

what does a kid
from Pennsylvania
know?
About death and terror and this life?
Nothing.
I cannot get my head around it.
It was so easy to forget
while I was prancing
around the kibbutz,
the orchard.
Even in Jerusalem,
these gravest of thoughts
never entered my head.
Then, the scenes from the news
seemed so far away.
Nadav, were you with him,
when it happened? I ask.
No, he answers,
his voice a monotone,
It was a Sunday morning.
We were in the army.
Oren was returning to the
base after going home for Shabbat.
I stayed at the base;
I had guard duty that weekend.

And then our other friend,
another soldier,
called me.
He was hurt, but not so badly.
But he said the fire . . .
>   *body parts*
>   *screaming*
and Oren—
Nadav breaks off,
staring through the windshield.
I turn and look out at the
yellowing trees and grass.
Nadav is somewhere else.
I suppose he's remembering.
I feel so sad for him.
He shouldn't have this to carry around.
For the rest of his life.
He shouldn't.
Kids at school get upset
because we lost a football game.
It's not like this.
I squeeze his hand.
Nadav turns to me.
His grin returns,

like a summer breeze,
his eyes glinting in the gathering darkness.

We drive on,
my hand over his.
Then he pulls off the road,
jerking the car around,
and parks sideways alongside
a log.
A wooden and glass,
well,
shack, really,
leans slightly to the right.
This is the best meat in the
north of Israel,
Nadav pronounces proudly.
We enter, and
the room is dark,
and I am surprised to see
that there are about ten tables
covered with rich fabric
in shades of chartreuse
and jade.
A large woman,

large in every conceivable
dimension, emerges from
a back room and
greets us at the door.
Nadav, shalom l'cha!
she bellows, her heavy
lips and nose
moving,
wobbling as she speaks.
Shalom, Orit. This is Sarah,
he introduces me.
You are American?
She turns to peer at me.
Yes.
Good, so you will have a good
dinner, a good Israeli dinner.
She claps her hands
gleefully and seats us by
a window covered with
a thick drape that matches
the table linens.
Nadav orders for both of us,
and Orit brings us each
a glass of water and a goblet
of ruby red wine.

Suddenly I feel very grown up.
And I realize,
Nadav *is* very grown up.
I am abruptly too aware of
how much older he is at
twenty-one.
What did you do in the army?
I ask.
*I was a medic in Golani. I fought
in Lebanon,* he tells me.
Do you know the Golani unit? he continues.
No, I reply.
*Golani are the bravest soldiers,
and also sometimes,
the stupidest.*
He sips his wine.
*The army,
it was fun sometimes,
but it was very hard.
Very hard.*
He glances away,
then quickly turns
and looks me in the eyes.
*I hated the army.
Why,* I ask,

amazed. *I mean,*
I'm sure it's probably
scary sometimes.
But this is your country.
Don't you want to fight for it?
I wish I had a country to fight for,
I tell him.
You do. It's called America,
he snorts.
No, it's not the same,
I argue.
This country gives you three years
to watch your friends die,
to wait for your own death.
And wicked things happen
here.
Ah, you wouldn't understand.
Nadav's face begins to grow red.
Then the food arrives.
Thick steaks,
oozing juices and blood,
mashed potatoes rich with gravy,
and the salad that I am beginning
to learn is omnipresent.
Cucumbers and tomatoes,

cut into chunky squares,
float in a sea of olive oil and
lemon juice.
Nadav eats slowly,
but I can tell he's
angry;
his cheek muscle twitches
in between bites.
I don't understand.
Doesn't he realize
how lucky he is?
Nadav, I'm sorry,
I start.
Never mind. You are
young, Sarah. I forget that
sometimes.
And how can you know
what it's like here?
Don't worry.
I will teach you.
He grins at me,
but something in my stomach
ties a knot.

FALLING IN LOVE

I have grown used to
waking up with the dawn,
working through the morning,
and spending the nights by a bonfire
      or river,
sleeping for three or four hours,
and doing it all over
and over again.
We have one day of rest,
Saturday,
Shabbat.
On those days, I explore.
I feel I am growing wilder like the
brambles
and lean
like the valley wolves.
I have given most of my clothes
and old belongings
over to the kibbutz closet.

No need for all those things.
And I feel lighter.
Nadav and I run around the kibbutz
barefoot and bear our calluses and
the sting of the sharp stones beneath our feet
like a badge of courage.
Our brown feet and
dirty knees
are pocked by
blades of grass
while we kneel in the meadow,
the tattoos of our toughness.
One day Nadav and I climb to the top
of the giant water tank
on the perimeter of the kibbutz.
We scale it like lizards,
agile green lizards,
and when we get to the top,
we lie down on our backs
and stare at the sky.
Blue spots on blue and white wisps of clouds,
the sky presses down on me
      but it doesn't hurt a bit
while I lie here on this warm
metal cistern.

Nadav and I are friends,
but sometimes he forgets
that is all we are,
and sometimes he tries to steal kisses.
We spend our afternoons together,
talking about television shows
and our parents
and all kinds of things.
I really love it here.
I'm not going back
to the States,
I tell him
oh-so-nonchalantly.
Why? Why would you ever leave
the U.S.? It's the best
place. You have there
everything, he says.
No, it's better here.
You just can't
understand
what I feel here.
How
being Jewish isn't
important anymore,
here,

and why that matters
to me,
I tell him.
What are you talking
about? It doesn't matter
if you are Jewish.
Here. There.
Who cares?
he answers.
I consider this—
how can Jewish not matter,
here of all places,
when so much of the warring
seems to be about
Jewish,
not Jewish?
      But that's just it.
The fighting,
it's over land.
Not religion.
And besides, it's easy for
Nadav to say Jewish
doesn't matter,
because everyone
he knows is Jewish

friends, teachers, grocers,
nurses, and soldiers.
He doesn't get it.
But he doesn't know a different life,
like I do.
You don't know what it's like
to be the only Jew in school,
how it feels when the kids
you've known your whole life
look at you
like you're a stranger
because you eat funny foods
or don't want to sing about
Jesus
and don't want to be wished
a merry Christmas
one
more
time.
You could never understand,
living here
all your life.
Where you've never been anything
but a part of the majority,

I say.
What's the difference?
You just be who you are.
Who cares about
Jewish or Christian? he prods.
You would, if
you weren't from here,
I tell him.
He just shakes his head
and rolls over onto his stomach.

I love to feel the soil under my fingers,
to know that I'm taking care of
my ancestors' homeland,
to know that what I'm doing is right.
I am free
for the first time
in sixteen years.
I have put tiny braids in my hair
like an Indian
      because I am a lady of the land
      now
and some flowers, too.
It hangs in tangles,

but I think it's perfect.
As I lie here on this warm, metal cistern,
the endless blue of the sky pressing down on me.

I have no idea what I want
except to stay here.
Forever?
Till September?
I don't worry about it.
I'm not burdened by
the cares and fears
of my old self.

Nadav and I slide down the ladder and
onto the brown earth again.
Then we race to the kibbutz garden
that overlooks the valley,
and we snatch figs from the trees,
tear at them with our teeth and devour them
like animals,
the sweet red juice
running over our hands,
down our arms.
We play in the swimming pool,
a pair of baby seals,

splashing and shrieking
and always laughing.
And then we eat our tomato and cucumber salads.
These are my days,
heady and sweet,
and they pass quickly
but blur into one another,
into one unending chain
of perfect,
easy
days.
I love it here.

SWALLOWED UP

I think of Jake and Lior
and how strong
and romantic
they seemed to me.
Kisses and crushes,
uniforms and guns,
checkpoints and football stadiums.
I don't know them.
They never really knew me.
Like Nadav does.
The day and a half
with Lior meant something,
but now I'm just not sure what.
He never called.
He never came to visit.
And I have surprised
myself by forgetting to be
sad.
Now Nadav and I hold

discussions of our plans for the future.
Not necessarily our plans together,
but that we will both be on the kibbutz.
This delicious freedom,
this peaceful adventure.
And my friend in this journey,
Nadav.

We're sitting on a wooden bench
in the garden,
watching the sun dip down below
the horizon.
It falls slowly to the crests of the hills
and sinks in
a flare of fuchsia and golden flames.
Faint lights appear
across the valley.
I can get you a day off
from work on Sunday,
he says to me,
out of the blue.
For what? I ask.
We could go camping
by the Kinneret,
the Sea of Galilee, he answers.

Camping?

Alone?

Together?

Okay, I tell him

shakily.

I walk slowly to my room,

passing the disorderly houses that

are graceful in their chaos,

and trees heavy with blossoms

that fly from their roots to grab

at my hair and scratch my arms.

Tomorrow night.

What will happen?

Where will our friendship go?

I go to bed, but I can't sleep.

I watch the stars

through the misty veil

of my curtains.

My stomach rumbles with

nerves.

I need somebody,

someone to talk to,

to tell me that

this will be all right.

That I'm not stupid
for trusting him,
for going with him.
I get up and walk around
behind my little
cabin room
and follow the path to the other
volunteer rooms.
I haven't walked around this area of the
kibbutz much,
but I find Katie's room
and gingerly knock
on her door.
Come in, she calls,
her voice questioning.
Hi, I say. *Is it
too late?*
Not at all. She looks
at me curiously and
pats the foot of her bed
for me to sit.
She is curled up against her pillow,
reading.
Her room looks exactly like mine,
undecorated, except

for some photographs.
Is this your family? I ask.
Yes.
Do you miss them?
Yes, I do. But
I had to get away, she says.
Her tone rings of finality,
and so I start to trace the lines
of the fabric in her blanket.
So, what's up? Katie asks.
Her face reveals only
mild curiosity.
I'm sorry to bother you. It's just,
well, I don't,
I don't trust the others so much,
and I just need to talk,
to ask you something.
I, I am not sure how to begin.
An outsider, always,
and here, even though
I was accepted, I still
feel drawn to the outcast.
Does that mean that I've
created this condition
for myself?

That no matter where I go,
it will be like this?
But Katie is kind,
and so maybe it's not
a bad thing.
Start at the beginning, Katie says.
Well, Nadav asked me to go camping
with him.
Alone.
And I'm afraid.
What are you afraid of? she asks me.
Aren't you two . . .
together?
I shake my head.
No.
I mean, sometimes he kisses me,
but we're friends.
I guess.
I don't know.
I'm so confused.
In high school the boys
ignore me, and then I come
to Jerusalem and meet someone
who turns out to be a jerk.
Then I come here and meet Nadav

and I like him a lot
and sometimes we kiss,
but I just don't know
what he wants,
what I want.
I don't know if I'm ready . . .
I'm leaving in a few weeks,
or maybe not.
I don't even know that.
But I've never
been alone with a boy
at night
and I'm not ready for this kind
of relationship.
There I've said it.
So don't do
anything you don't want to do,
she tells me.
Simple.
Just tell him.
It sounds easy,
but I am not inclined
to believe it
can be so.
What if I can't? I whisper.

You will be able to.
Listen to yourself.
> My voice,
> I want to hear it
> so badly.

You're not like the other girls here, she says.
No?
No.
I thank her and quietly
leave her room.
As I walk down the gravelly
path back to my room,
I watch the light of the moon
heighten and fade.
The sky darkens to its deepest black,
then daylight begins to reawaken.
My alarm isn't necessary tonight,
and I turn it off one minute before it is
set to ring.
It's Friday morning.

In the fields,
my body so weary,
I mechanically pull up the weeds,
numb to the beauty of the land.

The sad, lonely mountain is covered
with a heavy gray fog.
The morning sun is slow to make its way
across the sky.
It seems an unbearably long amount of time passes
before we go to breakfast,
where Nadav grins
and gives me a thumbs-up.
I return his smile, then
get up and walk to the bathroom
and lock the door,
my breath coming too quickly
to catch it.
I stand in front of the sink
and look at my
reflection in the mirror.
And look.
And look.
The features of my face
blur together
then crystallize for
a second. They
don't seem to be organic parts
of me.
They come apart, like

pieces
of

      a
   jigsaw
      puzzle.
A nose floats away,   unanchored
from my cheeks,
and there it is, just a nose,
a funny-looking thing
with two holes in it,
hanging in the air.
And a pair of gray-green eyes,
the color of mud,
but I only see one, as the two
merge in the center of my forehead
like a Cyclops.
Who am I?
What
am I doing?
Get it together.
It's just fun.
I wash my face
and go back outside.
The day goes and goes,
afternoon lingering,

then work is over, and I
run to my room,
fiddle around with my
hair in front of the
mirror.
These braids and
flowers and beads.
Do they think
I'm just a silly American,
acting the part of the native?
Can they see that I love it here,
that I belong here?

A JOURNEY

Like a prisoner walking to his
execution, I make my way to the
heder ochel.
And there he is, tall and dark
against the late afternoon sky.
He's so handsome, standing straight
and proud,
a lion,
yet lithe and graceful
as a gazelle.
He sees me coming, and his face
breaks into a sparkling
      yes, there's no other
      word to describe it
smile.
Suddenly, my feet start to skip
over the ground,
and I can't wait to be
close to him.

Hey, he says.

Hi. My voice comes out
breathyandlow,
and I'm surprised by how happy I am.
We need some blankets.
Let's get them
from the laundry room.
I think of Katie working in the laundry.
Okay.
Our feet crunch along the path
as I follow him to the laundry building
across from the dining hall.
Should I wait out here? I ask him.
He shakes his head,
and I take a breath
and trail after him into the laundry room.
I feel as though I'm
on autopilot
weaving among the tables for folding
and shelves piled with towels
and neatly creased blue jeans.
One of Beethoven's piano sonatas is playing
softly in the background.
Katie is bent over a large dryer,
pulling loads of laundry out,

filling a cart on wheels.

Katie?

She turns to look at us.

A question mark in her eyes,

Yes? Oh, hi, Sarah, Nadav.

Hey.

Suddenly I feel very embarrassed.

We need some sheets and blankets.

We are going camping,

Nadav says.

She stares at me closely,

then looks at Nadav.

Is that sternness in her eyes?

I'm not supposed to give you extra stuff,

especially not

to take out of the kibbutz.

She pauses.

But I'll give you some sheets.

I can't give you any blankets, though,

she tells us.

That's fine. Thank you so much,

I blurt out.

Just don't tell anybody, she says.

We won't. Promise. Thank you!

It's okay.

And she hands Nadav a small
pile of sheets that
smell of lemons and
the kibbutz air.
Have fun, she says.
I smile a small grateful smile at her,
and she winks and gives me a
knowing look.
Then we step out into the bright sunlight.
How will we get there? I ask.
*We'll take a bus from town. We have
to get some food at the store
anyway,* he says.
As we retrace our steps
to the parking lot,
a woman is readying to leave
and offers us a ride.
In town we find the small grocery store
and buy cans of corn,
bags of pita bread, hummus,
cucumbers, and something
Nadav picks up called *halvah,*
which he assures me I'll like.
On the bus,
Nadav holds my hand,

and it feels kind of
strange, as though
the air between
us is silently changing,
charging.
But I cannot get past
the barriers of my
own skin to understand this
budding transformation.
I must wait for the air
to envelop me and
dissolve into my pores,
then see what happens.
We roll down the winding hills
and the Kinneret comes into view.
As we drive along the coast,
Nadav and I sit in friendly silence,
and I am relieved
that I don't have to fight myself
to think of things to talk about.
After a while,
Nadav reaches up and presses the button
along the wall of the bus
to let the driver know
to make the next stop.

We heave our bags onto our shoulders,
clunk down the steps,
and jump out
into the warm air.
Nadav takes my hand again
and leads me across the street to
a mostly empty stretch of beach.
We throw our things down
onto the sand and
spread out one of the sheets.
At first I feel shy, but then
we race each other down the beach
into the water.
It's shallow for a long way,
but it is cool and feels good.
My feet sink into the
tiny shards of broken pebbles
and seashells at the
bottom of the sea.
Finally we get out to a place
where the water
comes up to our shoulders.
It feels like we've crossed almost
half the length
of the lake by now.

The mountain that I could see
from the fields
of Kfar Avivim
appears much closer now,
the slopes a dry summer brown,
and palm trees dot the shore.
Nadav dives under the surface, and I
follow him.
We swim farther out,
his strong arms taking long, sure strokes.
Are you hungry? he asks,
as his head breaks the surface again.
A little bit, I answer.
So we head back to the shore,
and Nadav begins pulling items
out of our grocery bags.
He brings out two pitas and the hummus,
and we take turns dipping the flat bread
into the smooth, salty spread.
Have you had hummus before? Nadav asks.
No,

      but I love it.
It's like the national Israeli food, he laughs.
Really?
Yeah, Israelis all have their favorite

hummus place,
and they argue about it.
It's like a sport here.
Is this good hummus? I ask,
looking at the plastic tub
we got at the store.
This? No, this is terrible hummus.
You have to go to a real place,
where it's homemade. My favorite
is from a restaurant
in Jaffa, an Arab city
next to Tel Aviv.
It's a tiny little place that most
Israelis don't know about,
or wouldn't go to
because they're afraid.
Or they hate
Arabs.
You go to Arab
restaurants? I ask him,
surprised.
Sure.
But . . . isn't it weird?
I don't know if I'm being stupid,
but I can't understand

how this country works.
How the Israelis know they're
going into the army
from the time they are born,
that they're going to fight
Arabs
       an enemy?
but here is Nadav, saying he eats
in an Arab restaurant.
Look, it's not like all Arabs
are bad, he tells me. *It's*
complicated. But I
wouldn't go to their parts of the city
in my army uniform.
It's hard when we're all
living so close to each other.
And they're not the only bad guys,
either,
he explains.
How could you have fought
in the army, if
you feel that way?
I ask him.
I had no choice, he says.
And that is that.

There are still so many things about this place
that just don't make sense to me,
that I don't know about.
How can I say with such certainty
that Israel is my home
when I know so little?
When the kibbutz keeps me safe
from everything outside
its yellow gates?
It's starting to grow dark, and Nadav
and I set about spreading the sheets
around, to make a little campground
for ourselves.
We ball up our clothes in our bags to
use as pillows, and I gather driftwood
and yellowed palm fronds
for Nadav to make a fire.
We sit by the flames
and make more hummus sandwiches,
and Nadav cuts the cucumbers into cubes
with his pocket knife,
and we add them to our pita.
Then we open one of the cans of corn.
The kernels break between my teeth

in a burst of sweet juice,
and it's just about the most delicious
thing I've ever eaten.
Nadav smiles at me over the fire,
the flames flickering in his dark pupils.
Tell me,
why did you hate the army? I ask.
You want to know so much
about the army, he says, shaking his head.
Mostly it was okay. You know . . .
his voice trails off.
No, I really don't know,
I break in.
Well, most of the time we just
hung around our base
and smoked cigarettes and talked about girls.
Did you have a girlfriend? I ask.
He looks confused
for a second.
No, we didn't talk about
real girls, he says,
smiling again.
Then, sometimes, we had
to fight.

And those times were awful.
Some guys love playing soldier,
shooting their guns,
bragging about who they hit,
but I think they do that because
they're scared.
He grows quiet again,
staring out at the water,
as though he is reliving something,
and I'll never know what.
Enough. Let's not talk about
these sad things.

KINNERET

A few yards away, another group
of Israeli teenagers is also camping out,
and one of them is playing
a guitar.
The song is a sad one,
and the crying strains of the
strings
drift over to us.
Come, let's go in the water.
Nadav stands, pulling me up
beside him.

    But it's dark. . . .
That's the best part, he says.
Don't worry,
I'll hold your hand.

    You won't get lost.
The water is warmer now.
We wade towards the middle of the lake.
Float, Nadav instructs me.

He turns onto his back,
eyes tilted towards the sky.
I follow his lead,
lie on the water
and stare up at the sky.
There are so many stars.
I've never seen such a sky,
blanketed with specks of light,
and the moon hanging
in the middle of it all,
casting a ghostly glow across the lake.
I lie there, feeling the water
brush against my ears,
a hollow sound,
its warmth lapping over my body,
rhythmically pushing and pulling me back.
It can carry me wherever it likes.
I feel a part of the water, a piece of the sea.
    My flesh, my cells turn to water,
    to be washed away by the tide.

Seconds pass.

My arms and hands tingle.
I stare up at the sky

and the stars
suspended
in their inky night
appear closer than they ever have before.
The weight of the sky
presses down on my body.
Presses with heavenly strength.
And I lie here,
floating on water,
my liquid frame
crushed by the sky.
Breath is hard to find.

Silently I gasp,
a land creature trapped at sea.
I feel as empty as the shells beneath the water,
lost in the vastness of sea
and sky.
But my toes touch the shells
that coat the seafloor,
and I find my footing
on the empty houses
of creatures who have
long since vacated the premises.
I think with envy

of these creatures,
who so easily
shed their homes for new ones.
Family, friends, religion,
none of these
questions,
weights
to burden them.

      Not like me.

I reach down,
fingers brushing the sand,
digging and scraping
until they find the smooth, rounded
form of a seashell.
I pick it up and examine
its exquisite coils,
rub its cool hardness
illuminated by the moon.
In the silvery light,
the exterior glistens like a pearl.

      Bone and sand.

Oh, what am I doing here
in this place
I don't actually know.
I can't go home. I can't go back there.

Here, I feel free.
And there, there is nothing,
but the droning of bees
  get into the right college
  get good grades
  don't be such a nerd
and I don't want any of it.
Nobody asks what I want.
They don't care.
They have it all figured out,
for me.
But I don't.

HIDING

I make the decision to forget
it all.
Nadav and I
play in the water.
The first night and second day pass quickly.
On the second night,
we bid good-bye to the Kinneret.
We stay in the sea too long,
and our fingers and toes are
colorless and wrinkled
when we emerge,
seaweed tangled in my hair,
to go with the braids and beads,
the flowers since washed away.
But the campfire and
some grapefruit soda
recall the life back to our
limbs.
Nadav unwraps the halvah,

which is a short block
the color of concrete.
He cuts a piece with
his knife
and hands it to me.
Here, try this, he tells me,
holding it out like an offering in his hand.
I take the morsel and more pieces
fall
and I put it on top of my tongue.
The halvah has a sweet, nutty flavor,
warm and crumbly,
and it melts against the roof of my mouth.
My eyes widen,
and I look at Nadav with delight.
He is looking at me intently,
expectantly.
It's wonderful, I exclaim.
And he grabs me so quickly,
and pushes his lips against mine,
and we are kissing and pulling each
other's hair,
and my head is dizzy,
I can't think,
only tug and touch and taste.

Sarah, he breathes.

You are wonderful.

I pull away to look at him.

His eyes are wide,

and his gaze is cast downward.

Don't go back to America,

he whispers.

Stay here.

Could it be?

Do I have this power

over a boy?

To make him want me,

to make him love me?

I will, I reply.

Stay with me, Sarah.

I reach for his face,

rubbing his rough cheeks,

and kiss him again.

He snatches at my T-shirt, and suddenly,

the petals of this perfect flower

shrivel

and fall away.

He wants too much.

No, Nadav.

I like you

so much,
but
I'm not ready,
I whisper, pulling
at his hands.
He fights me,
then sits back, an annoyed
look on his face.

Is he mad?

No, contrite.
He runs his fingers through his hair
and looks out at the sea.
Okay, Sarah. And he kisses me,
then lies back on the sheets.
His eyes close, the moon casting
her ghostly light over
his face, and I lean
over him and kiss his lips.

He is perfect.
His hand reaches up and
brushes my cheek, and I'm
thrown into a spinning
tornado of
sensations.
My stomach is jumping all

around, and I'm so confused.
These sensations scare me,
and I know,
not now.

This is my adventure.
Someone sees me.
I'm not doomed
to invisibility
forever.
My body is not deformed,
my mind not empty
and dull.
I have found my voice here
and filled my skin with my own sounds.
And they are worth hearing.

The next morning
we pack up our things
and wait for the bus in the sun.
Nadav kisses me over and over,
taking long looks,
as though he is drinking in
the features of my face,
storing them in his memory

for later.
We ride back to the kibbutz
in each other's arms,
not speaking,
and I finally understand
the change that was ready
to burst into being
two days before.
Nadav whispers that I should
come to his mother's house
and taste her couscous,
and we can go to Tel Aviv together,
and he'll show me everything.
And yet,
even while we talk of these things,
a part of me,
the deepest part of my heart,
fears that these plans
will never come to pass,
that these are wasted words.
And so I bury them
like a golden treasure.

ROUNDING IT OUT

Dawn.
It's Monday morning,
and I wake up again
and return to work,
and I'm sleepy
but glad to fall back
into the routine.
At breakfast, I see Nadav,
and when he glances at me,
his face lights up.
After lunch, I find
Katie hanging around near
our bunks,
and I thank her
and ask if she wants to take a walk.
She looks surprised,
but accepts.
I lead her around the twisting paths
of the kibbutz

to the place where I first found the bomb shelter.
This is the best view of the kibbutz,
from up here. And I start
to hoist myself up
to the top of the dome-shaped structure.
She looks up dubiously, then shrugs
and begins climbing.
When she reaches the top,
she sits heavily, looks out
over the houses and land,
and she sighs.
What are you thinking right now? I ask her.
She is startled by my question,
but then she smiles.
I'm thinking about how beautiful
this place is, and how little
time I've taken to
really look at it.
But you've looked.
She pauses.
And I was wondering
how your weekend was,
she giggles.
It is nice to see Katie laugh.
She has a pretty smile.

It was fun.

Perfect, really.

So, what happened? she asks.

I lean close to her.

I think I have an

Israeli boyfriend.

That's nice, she says.

So, it was okay?

Yes, I reply.

It was okay.

She nods, and her gaze

has turned wistful.

I put my hand over hers and

give it a little squeeze.

What is it? I ask.

She looks at me gratefully and smiles.

I know I haven't been very friendly here,

she says.

It's just so hard

for me to . . .

Her voice breaks off,

and she is

wiping tears from her eyes

with the back of her hand.

It's okay, I tell her.

I came here to forget
about someone, she says.
A man? I ask.
She nods.
Everyone thought we should
be together. He did,
our parents,
our friends.
Everyone but me.
And I told him
and them,
then I left
because they were so
angry with me.
But I had to,
had to make them hear me.
You did the right thing, I tell her,
and you were brave.
I put my arm around her shoulders.
We sit there and watch the sun
finish the day's journey
and set,
spilling darkness
over the fields.

A DESERT BULLET

As I sit in the dining hall,
Nadav is close to me,
not touching me.
I cut my cucumber and tomato,
dinner after another day
in the fields.
Adi runs over to me and says
there is a call for me on
the pay phone downstairs.
I can't imagine who it is.
I've never received a phone call
here, in all these weeks.
I start to worry that something
has happened at home.
I haven't been calling my parents
very regularly.
I run to the stairs,
looking back to catch
Nadav shooting me a

concernedconfused
look.
I lock myself in the phone
closet and pick up the
receiver, which Adi has
left lying on its side.
Hello? I ask.
Sarah?
Michal's voice fills the
receiver, teary and shaking.
Michal? What's wrong?
What happened?
Sarah, something happened.
Something happened.
My thoughts fly like a balloon
leaking its helium.
Did something happen
to one of my parents?
Is one of the boys in trouble?
Hurt?
Michal, tell me.
My heart begins to
thump wildly.
Please!
She drags in a breath.

Assaf is in the hospital, and Lior . . .
It's Lior.
He was shot.
The balloon deflates
and lands tangled in
a tree.
Caughtconfused.
What?
Lior was killed.
What?
I don't understand.
He was killed, Sarah.
Her voice breaks.
Suddenly, everything comes
into crisp focus.
Is Assaf okay? I ask.
Focus.
Focus.
The graffiti on the
walls of this booth,
hearts filled with
Hebrew initials
in red and black marker,
the painted numbers
on the phone are

chipped, faded from
the touch of so many fingers.
Is Assaf okay? I
repeat to her sobs.
Yes, he's safe. But
he is in the hospital
for shock.
He was next to Lior when
it
happened.
It.
Avi and I are leaving
to go to him,
but I wanted to tell you so
you didn't hear it
on the news.
Sarah, are you all right?
Her voice
cloudy with saltwater tears.
Yes, yes I'm okay.
Don't worry, just
go to Assaf.
I love you, I say.
I hang up and
crouch on the floor.

My breath comes quickly,
too quickly,
and my heart
still pounds.
Squatting and shaking,
I try to think.
The clarity has vanished,
left me alone with
        an emptiness.
I remember his long, graceful
fingers,
warm and rough.
How can I understand?
I'll never see them again.
Face it,
        I wouldn't have
seen them again anyway.
But those hands won't be
in the world,
touching other girls,
won't hold anyone else's
hands.
And that's what gets me to cry,
to shiver and hiccup

on the floor of this phone booth.
The walls start to move, closer
and closer, squeezing
me to death.
But no, because,
I'm still alive, right?
I drag myself to my
feet and out of the stale,
little closet.
The fresh air jolts me
so I imagine I feel
the blood coursing through
my veins.
Not like Lior's blood,
a crimson stain
on the earth
or a white hospital sheet.
Dead.
Killed in action.
This country,
this place.
The rose-colored window
has cracked.
How could I have been so arrogant

to believe that this was
my home?
      I am a coward.
I wanted it so badly, though.
To live here
and be happy here.
I thought I could escape Pennsylvania
and leave that life behind
forever.
I thought I'd found
a place,
a land
that was mine.
It all makes sense now.
Nadav's words,
how I didn't get it.
He hates the army;
      this could have
      been him.
He hates all that living in this
country has taken from him.
And I was blind to it.
Pebbles crunch beneath my bare feet,
sharp and cool.
I breathe in deeply.

The air is fragrant and heavy.
Soft and warm, it touches my
face, trying to comfort me with
a gentle caress.
Dread rises like bile,
fills my heart, my stomach, my throat.
I'm choking on dread.
The lights in the houses
glow with a warmth and a peace
that I had once,
that I kept in my pocket.
That I kept there
for my own
like a secret.
But now,
I think
maybe it was never mine.
And when I go back, it will be over.
I will wake up
to different sky, different air, different land.
And this dream will be over.
The fairy tale will end
and I'll be taunted, tormented
by the flooding memories and tears.

§ § §

There's a dirt path that travels through a place I love,
littered with stones and bomb shelters.

 I don't think
 it is home any longer.
I long for my mother
and the safety of the spot
in the crook of her neck,
where my nose fit just
perfectly
when I was small.
When we still cuddled.
When we didn't argue all the time.
When we were still close.
When her scent was home.

A FAREWELL?

My wanderings have led
me to Nadav's front door.
I knock, knowing
he has waited up for me.
Sarah. His eyes filled
with worry and tenderness.
What happened? You disappeared.
A . . . a friend of mine,
someone I met in Jerusalem,
was killed, I tell him.
Oh. Who? Where?
A friend of my cousin's.
They are—they were
      yes, past tense,
      how strange
in the army together.
My cousin is in the hospital, too,
for shock.
Nadav pulls me inside,

guides me to a chair and
brings a glass
of water from his small kitchen.
His look of pity or sympathy wrings
tears from my
eyes again.
Suddenly I feel as
though I'm watching
myself, us, this
tableau of melodrama
unfold on a life-sized movie screen.
There's that word again.
Life.
The first boy to hold my hand.
So final.
So final.

*Nadav, I think I should
go home,* I say after a moment.
I'll walk you, he offers.
*No, I mean back to
the States.*
What?
He begins to stalk around the apartment,
circling,

like a tiger in a cage. *Why?*
This place, this country
it's not for me.
But you love it here, he pleads.
I did. I do, I say. *But*
you were the one telling
me all the time that I didn't
understand what living here
means, the burden. I
understand now.
His eyes flash. *But if you*
love a place

      or a person,

he looks at me closely,
dares me silently
to hold his gaze,
you take the good and the bad
together.
But what if I can't take the bad?
What if I can't handle it?
I'm thinking, give me a reason.
Just one.
You can handle it, Sarah.
I know you.
Things happen—

bad things can happen
anywhere.
No, things like this don't
happen in America.
But you said, he growls, *you'd never*
felt this happy
there.
I didn't. But this—
this is horrible. I don't
even know what
they're fighting for.
It's not my fight.
No, he says, *it's not my fight*
either. But
here I am.
Nadav, you were the one
who was always saying
how great America
is. How you hate
living here.
Now you've changed your mind?
I shout at him.
Suddenly the room is charged with an angry intensity.
He glowers at me
and I see his

jaw working,
the telltale muscle in his
cheek twitching.
So that's it? You'll
just run away? he spits.
I'm only supposed to be here another two
weeks anyway, I throw back at him.
Fine, he says.
And he turns away,
stomping into his bedroom.
Fine, I whisper.
I rise from his tatty chair
and let myself out.
The warm, heavy
air, now still
with late-at-night
silence,
brushes my arms
and cheeks.
I make my way back to
my room and close the door.

THE END

~

Two weeks pass.
They pass quickly,
like all the days before.
But during these weeks,
a gray dullness
washes away the joy.

Wake at dawn,
trudge
mechanically
     arms and legs
     swinging like a robot
to the dining hall.
Coffee burns and churns in my stomach.
In the fields I pull up the
weeds, an automaton.
The hawks and wolves
are there,
but I don't see,

don't hear them.
Bonfires after dinner
and trips to the river,
but sometimes I stay
in my room and read,
instead.
Today, my last day
in the fields.
No hawks or wolves.
And at breakfast I eat
carrots with my
cucumbers.
It's fitting to feel like this,
        an outsider
again,
eating the ostracized carrot
at breakfast.
The orange sweetness
comforts me in
a way. In that
carrot way.
I see Shmuel jump on the
tractor, and I
climb up to
join the others.

Sarah, he asks,
you are okay?
Yes, I answer.
I will be. Thank you.
He smiles his shy smile and
drives us back down to the fields.
The other girls look
at me questioningly.
But I am silent.
At lunch Katie sits
beside me,
casting worried glances
my way.
Sarah, is everything
all right? she asks.
Yeah. I'm just thinking
about all the packing
I have to do, I lie.
Nadav avoids looking at me.
As he has done since
the night I found out about
Lior's death.
Everything changed after
that night.

After lunch,
I stay in my work clothes,
sticky though they are,
and I follow the
tractor trail
down to the cornfield
to say my good-bye
to the land
in private.
　　　Then I hear it.
The language of wolves.
It's not a strange
sound to me anymore
and I welcome it.
Good-bye, wolves,
I hear myself murmur.
And the edge of the
grayness is tinged with
a rosy hue.
I do love it here.
I sneak back to the dining
hall and fill my pockets
with carrots, cucumbers,
and bread, and I secret

them away to my room.
As the sun begins to set,
I step outside and
walk around to Katie's room.
I knock on her door and enter
at her answering call.
I just came to say good-bye.
Thanks for everything, I tell her.
You're off? Well,
have a safe trip,
and thank you, too.
Good luck with everything, I say
before turning around and closing
her door behind me.
I step back into the gathering twilight
and find myself on the path
that leads to the bomb shelter.
Once again,
I scale the stones
and perch on the rounded top.
I watch the sky turn purple
and pink and bathe
the land in dusky shadows.
My land.
God, it's so beautiful.

§ § §

There you are.
I spin around and see Nadav
standing below,
smiling up at me.
He hoists himself
up and sits beside me.
It's your last night,
isn't it? he says.
I nod and look away.
I'm sorry I was a jerk, he says.
I'm sorry, too.
Are you happy to go back? he asks.
Not really.
I've sort of turned off. . . .
I don't know what I feel or
think
anymore.
Nadav turns a half grin
on me.
I'm glad I met you.
I'm glad I met you, too, I tell him.
He puts his arm around my
shoulder, and I turn
to face into him.

We embrace, and
it is strange how
I don't feel that tug
of electricity connecting
us any longer.
And I know he is
noticing the same thing.
The romance has ended.
But Nadav was always a good friend.
You'll keep in touch? I ask him.
Of course.
He lets go and we smile
and he slides down,
turns, and waves.
Then he disappears
around a corner
in the gray gravelly
path.
A sigh and a final look around,
then I jump down and
make my way back to my room.
There I see, from my bed,
a small, wooden night table
and a glowing clock with an alarm

I have learned not to hear
at 4:30 in the morning.
The heat is sweltering,
but I sleep with the covers on
anyway.
Outside, wolves howl,
and the moon shines down on me
through the little square of window,
bathing me in her light.
The sun will return soon, bringing the
hour of my departure
with it.
It is time to go.
Time to leave this land of
beautiful dreams
and nightmares.

UPON MY RETURN

I wake up to America
and my parents' love.
They smothered me
with coddling
and concerned glances
for a week or so,
but now they expect me to
snap out of it,
        out of my *funk*,
as they call it.
I call it
        misery.
I don't feel
funky,
that's for sure.
I am back in school,
my senior year.
The rigid wooden chairs
connected to

sad wooden desks
that dig into my knees
constrict and cage me.
The shabby greens
and mustard yellows
of the cement walls
mock
the verdance of the fields.
Lines and logarithms
and equations of
calculus confine
my mind, and not even
the music of marching band
can unlock me.
During practice we hutt, two, three, four.
Right left right left right.
It's all a droning drain of
sameness.
Hutt, two, three, four
Hutt, two, three, four
Right left right left right.
Not even the music of my friends
can unlock me.
They cannot understand what
this summer was like.

Nothing has changed here
but me.
Though my friends are still my friends,
something is different.
I've left them behind.
Alice and Annie play duets,
and it's okay,
because the reedy sound
reminds me of the sea
turning over stones
and shells,
of feet crunching on gravel.
　　　Here, it will always be like this.

How can a patch of land
mean so much?
But then, I guess that's the
key, isn't it.
To all of it.

PENNSYLVANIA

Homecoming.
The marching band is
balanced on the bleachers,
clarinet crossed over my lap.
The football players
scurry like ants over the field,
and the cheerleaders
jump and screech like crickets.
Alice nudges me.
Jake looks so cute, huh?
I guess, I reply.
You could ask him to dance
at the dance
tonight, she continues.
I don't think so, I tell her.
Jake is still
the most popular boy,
the cutest boy
in school.

He runs around on his
skinny legs and
throws the ball
and jumps through the
hoops placed in front of him.
And suddenly,
all of the reasons I worshipped him,
all of the years before this one,
come crashing down
like a house of cards.
He does what he is told
and nothing more.
He follows the orders of his coach
and his teachers
and his girlfriend.
And he doesn't see
all of the possibilities
that float all around him.

I do.

THE ANNOUNCEMENT

One night at dinner,
I am pushing my carrots
        steamed with butter and tarragon
around on my plate,
and my mother notices my fidgetiness,
and she asks,
So, Sarah,
did you make a decision yet?
Brown?
Penn?
There is a hint of giddiness
behind her words.
She has been waiting for
this moment
my whole life.
My crowning achievement.
        Or hers?
Actually, I have, I reply.
I take a breath.

I've decided not to go
to Brown or Penn, I begin.
What! my mother shouts.
Well, I applied to Hebrew University
in Jerusalem and I decided to go there.
I got the acceptance letter last week.
My mother drops her fork.
What? she shrieks again.
You're going to waste your life.
How can you give up
the opportunity to
go to an Ivy League university?
What will you do in Israel?
Where would you stay?
My mother's shoulders have started
to heave.
Her breath is coming in gasps.
Mom, I'll live in the dorms,
and Michal will be close by.
I'm fighting to stay calm.
David, say something, she yells at my father.
He looks at me and then at her
and says, *I expected this*
months ago,
quite frankly.

I look at him in
surprise.
His beard is sprinkled
with so much gray, I notice.
Or maybe I haven't
really looked at him
in a long time.
My mother stares at him and shakes
her head,
lips pursed tight,
so tight.
You're just going to
let her
throw everything away?
My mother is really yelling now,
and she's just getting started.
Mom, I'm not throwing anything away.
This is what I want to do,
I interrupt.
My father slowly brings his
fork
down
to the table.
Diane, don't be ridiculous.
Hebrew University is

an excellent school,
and if this is what she wants,
I will not stop her.
      You're not going to Israel,
      she shouts at me.
Now she is crying.
And I'm waiting for my father to tell me
to look what I've done to my mother,
but he doesn't.
He's sitting there,
his hand splayed on the tabletop,
and he stares at me calmly.
She should go, he says quietly
to my mother.
But she'll be so far
away,
and she won't want
to come back, she whimpers.
Yes, she'll be far. My father
looks at me, his
lips struggling
between a smile and
sadness.
Mom, Dad, I love you.

But I love it there, too.
     I belong there.
I promise you,
it won't feel so far.
I promise.
Okay, my mother whispers, closing her eyes.
My father nods
and I rise to embrace
the two of them.
This is it.
The end of the discussion.
I'm going back to Israel.
Thank you, I tell them.
I run outside
and lie down on the
freshly cut grass.
The sky filled
with its stars
hangs above,
but its weight
doesn't press down
on me.
It hums and glows and
makes me feel light.

A sense of hope has
settled over me.
My hometown is a small
place
and the heel rubs.
But I strive to be like the snail,
who carries his home with him,
who carries it in his heart.

And although I know
it can't be,
I imagine I hear
the singing of the wolves.